"We're not kids

"I know," Brody replied quietly. can't talk."

"No." Irena couldn't seem to pull her eyes away from his lips. "It doesn't."

She was standing as close to him as a heartbeat. She could feel his breath on her face when he spoke. The feel of his breath on her skin stirred her.

Was she just being needy again?

Was she missing Ryan, struggling to put his memory to rest?

No, it wasn't that. She'd made peace with all that. This was something else, something different.

All she knew was that she was very, very attracted to the man she had always considered her best friend.

Had it been there all along, waiting to be discovered?

Dear Reader,

It's been two years since we were last in Hades, Alaska. At the time, I was pretty certain that it was the last book I was writing about the citizens of the feisty little town. But, as with all those rock stars who are coming out of retirement only to hit the road again in yet another "last tour," revisiting the songs they love, last doesn't necessarily mean last. Hades keeps giving birth to interesting situations, pulling me (and hopefully you) back for yet another look. This time it's to watch the story of Yuri Yovich's granddaughter unfold. Irena Yovich left Hades eighteen years ago, after discovering the man she planned to spend the rest of her life with in bed with one of her friends. Hurt and angry, she turned that into positive energy and became a top-flight lawyer with an exclusive law firm in Seattle. She's back in Hades, an event she thought would never happen, to attend her ex-lover's funeral. While in Hades, she reconnects with friends from her childhood, including Brody Hayes, her best friend as well as her ex-lover's brother. What she doesn't know is that Brody has been in love with her for as long as he's known her. But enlightenment is just around the corner.

I hope you enjoy this latest tale from the 49th state and, as ever, I wish you someone to love who loves you back.

With thanks,

Marie Ferrarella

MARIE FERRARELLA

Loving the Right Brother

SPECIAL EDITION®

Published by Silhouette Books

America's Publisher of Contemporary Romance

SILHOUETTE BOOKS

ISBN-13: 978-0-373-65459-8

LOVING THE RIGHT BROTHER

PLEASE RECYCLE

THIS PRODUCT IS RECYCLABLE

Recycling programs
for this product may
not exist in your area.

Visit Silhouette Books at www.eHarlequin.com

Printed in U.S.A.

Books by Marie Ferrarella

Silhouette Special Edition

††*Her Good Fortune* #1665
‡*Because a Husband is Forever* #1671
‡‡*The Measure of a Man* #1706
‡*She's Having a Baby* #1713
‡*Her Special Charm* #1726
Husbands and Other Strangers #1736
§*The Prodigal M.D. Returns* #1775
°*Mother in Training* #1785
Romancing the Teacher #1826
§§*Remodeling the Bachelor* #1845
§§*Taming the Playboy* #1856
§§*Capturing the Millionaire* #1863
°°*Falling for the M.D.* #1873
~*Diamond in the Rough* #1910
~*The Bride with No Name* #1917
~*Mistletoe and Miracles* #1941
††*Plain Jane and the Playboy* #1946
~*Travis's Appeal* #1958
§*Loving the Right Brother* #1977

Silhouette Romantic Suspense

*In Broad Daylight #1315
*Alone in the Dark #1327
*Dangerous Disguise #1339
~~The Heart of a Ruler #1412
*The Woman Who
  Wasn't There #1415
*Cavanaugh Watch #1431
†Her Lawman on Call #1451
†Diagnosis: Danger #1460
**My Spy #1472
†Her Sworn Protector #1491
*Cavanaugh Heat #1499
†A Doctor's Secret #1503
†Secret Agent Affair #1511
*Protecting His Witness #1515
Colton's Secret Service #1528
The Heiress's 2-Week Affair #1556

*Cavanaugh Justice
~~Capturing the Crown
†The Doctors Pulaski
**Mission: Impassioned
††The Fortunes of Texas: Reunion
‡The Cameo
‡‡Most Likely To…
§The Alaskans
°Talk of the Neighborhood
§§The Sons of Lily Moreau
°°The Wilder Family
~Kate's Boys

MARIE FERRARELLA

This *USA TODAY* bestselling and RITA® Award-winning author has written over one hundred and fifty novels for Silhouette Books, some under the name Marie Nicole. Her romances are beloved by fans worldwide. Visit her Web site at www.marieferrarella.com.

To
Gail Chasan,
for being kind enough
to include me in this
celebration of families
and for always being
such a mensch.

Chapter One

There was wilderness everywhere she looked. For all intents and purposes, civilization had vanished since she'd left Anchorage.

Nothing's changed. Except for me.

After all this time, it seemed odd to return to a place she'd sworn she'd never set foot in again. A place that she had spent the first eighteen years of her life dreaming about leaving. And when she finally had, there'd been tears. Tears that had nothing to do with anticipated nostalgia.

They were the kind of tears generated by a broken heart.

In a way, it was a little like trying on an old sweater you knew you no longer wanted. Even so, the familiar feel of it against your skin evoked bittersweet memories you were heretofore certain you had either forgotten or at least successfully blocked out of your mind.

She didn't want to remember.

But wasn't that why she was coming back? Because she remembered?

Irena Yovich stared out the window, watching Hades, Alaska, growing from a speck to a 500-citizen town as one of the several "taxiplanes" owned by Kevin Quintano and his wife, June, drew closer.

The young woman piloting the small passenger plane was June Yearling, the best damn mechanic for two hundred miles the year that Irene had left Hades for Seattle and college. Everyone in Hades knew that if it had an engine, June could fix it. And now, according to what June was saying on this hundred-mile run from Anchorage to Hades, she was not only a successful businesswoman but she was a wife and a mother of two, to be expanded to three in the not-too-distant future.

June had been her best friend once. She'd been one of the very few who hadn't gone behind her back to betray her. Possibly the only one, Irena thought with a trace of cynicism born in the wake of her rude awakening ten years ago.

"But when I heard you needed a ride from the airport, I told Kevin there was no way anyone else but me was flying the plane to bring you to Hades. He likes to give me a hard time because he doesn't think a woman in my condition should be piloting a plane, but I got him to give in." June ended with a gleeful, triumphant laugh. Her voice swelled with affection as she added, "Kevin's really a good guy."

Undoubtedly the last of a dying, if not dead, breed, Irena thought.

Since, as far as she could see, her friend wasn't showing and, more to the point, when June had thrown her arms around her and hugged her, June's stomach hadn't made contact first, she couldn't help asking, "Just how far along are you?"

"Only three months," June tossed over her shoulder, then added, in a somewhat quieter voice, "and four weeks."

Irena felt just the slightest bit of a smile touch her lips. June always had a way of twisting things in her favor. "Unless my math's totally off, that's actually four months."

June sighed dramatically. "I know, I know, but I just had to see if it was you or someone else with the same name."

Irena laughed out loud for the first time since she had gotten her grandfather's phone call yesterday morning, telling her that Ryan Hayes was dead by his own hand. Thanks to June, some of the tension drained from her.

Temporarily.

"And just how many Irena Yoviches could there be?" she asked her old friend.

She saw June's shoulders rise and fall beneath her fur-lined parka. "In Alaska, maybe not all that many, but in Russia, who knows? There's no telling, but one of them might have wanted to check out a place that was named after hell and is frozen over for six months out of the year, cut off from the rest of the world except for our little passenger service. And the doctors' planes, of course. Did I tell you that April's married to a doctor?" June said, referring to her older sister. "Jimmy's Kevin's younger brother," she added quickly. "He came to Hades to visit their sister Alison. She's a nurse here— and married to Jean Luc. Max married their sister Lily. They met when she came up here to visit, too. Come for a visit and stay forever. We're thinking of making it a city motto," June teased.

God, the people in Hades certainly had been busy, getting married and having lives, Irena thought. It made her feel out of sync, even though she knew that when it came to a successful career, she undoubtedly had them all beat. But as of late, her career hadn't been nearly the comfort it had been at first.

"Well, it's me," she said to June. "Does that make it worth the white lie you told your husband when you bent the truth?"

"Oh, Kevin's pretty good at math," June assured her. "Among other things."

Irena's view of June was restricted to the back of the latter's blond head; but by the sound of it, there was a satisfied, mischievous smile on June's lips.

"Good for you," Irena said, genuinely happy for the way her friend's life had turned out.

"So, how about you?" June pressed. "Are you married or anything yet?"

Ah, the question her mother managed to work into the conversation every time she called, Irena thought.

"No, I'm not 'married or anything yet.' And before you ask, there's nobody special at the moment."

She'd thrown in the last three words as camouflage. Despite the fact that she'd actually been engaged for a while a few years ago—a mistake from the moment she'd said "yes"—there hadn't been anyone really special in her life. Not since Ryan. Even that had turned out to be a lie. Ryan had never been the person she'd thought he was.

No, she upbraided herself sternly. He'd turned out to be exactly the person she'd thought he was. She'd just believed he'd changed for her. God, how could she have been so naive? From the moment he'd hit puberty, Ryan Hayes had been the Hades resident "bad boy," so good-looking that it'd been impossible for any female with a pulse to look at him without feeling instant infatuation.

In a state where there were seven men for every woman, Ryan Hayes had far more than his share of adoring females available to him. Tall, dark, with incredible green eyes and a look that made hearts pound wildly, he had been as faithful as a honeybee in the middle of spring, flying from one willing flower to the next. But for a while—three years to be exact—she'd believed Ryan when he had sworn that he was being faithful to her.

She'd believed him when he'd promised to go away with her to college. She remembered how proud of herself she'd been. Ryan was two years older than she was, and he'd had no intentions of furthering his education. She actually thought she'd talked him into it.

She'd believed him when he told her that he'd been accepted by the same university that she had. Believed him even though he remained evasive whenever she asked to see his acceptance letter.

What an idiot she'd been. But she'd wanted to believe in him—in *them*—so much that, in hindsight, she'd stubbornly overlooked so many of the telltale signs. She'd thought that others, envious of Ryan's looks and his money, were telling lies about him in an effort to break them up.

She went right on believing that they were destined for a fairy tale life and that everything was going to work out for the best. Until the night she walked in on him and Trisha Brooks without a stitch of clothing between them, obviously consumed with the intent to create their own fire.

As she ran out, she could almost literally feel her heart breaking within her chest. Stunned, she wasn't sure which of them she'd been angrier with—Trisha who had always maintained that she was one of her closest friends or Ryan, to whom she'd given her heart and her soul as well as her body.

In the end, she forgave Trisha because she knew firsthand how persuasive Ryan could be, how just being around him could make a woman forsake her common sense. But she refused to forgive Ryan. She finally admitted that she had been deluding herself all that time about their future together. There *was* no future. Coming to grips with that hurt like hell, because, even though she'd initially tried to resist, she'd wound up loving him with all her heart.

And she still loved him. An ache filtered all through her. Despite her ambitions, her goal to become a top-flight criminal lawyer, her young world had revolved around Ryan. He was the center of everything for her.

Once she realized that he didn't love her the way she loved him, her sense of loss was almost overwhelming. In the days that followed her discovery, she went into a tailspin, simultaneously numb and in agony. A sense of indifference came over her, holding her prisoner. She was going to give it all up—her ambitions, her dreams of being a lawyer, college, everything. Not to remain with Ryan, she knew there was no way that was going to happen, but because she'd lost her drive, her spark, her very focus.

It was her grandfather, Yuri, who sat down with her and slowly, patiently, talked her back to the land of the living. And it was Yuri who, filled with pride and together with her mother, came to see her graduate with top honors three years later. And again three years after that when she graduated from law school.

She'd fast-tracked her studies for both her undergraduate and her law degree. She deliberately excluded everything and anything that didn't have to do with her studies. For six years, she didn't have a personal life outside of those times when her grandfather and her mother came to visit her. It was the only way she could get over Ryan.

After law school, she'd gone to work at one of the most prestigious law firms in Seattle, Farley & Roberson. When her mother, Wanda, realized that she was never coming back to Hades, she had moved down to Seattle to be with her. Shortly after her move, Wanda, having lost her husband to a mining accident more than twenty years ago, met someone. A year later, she was Mrs. Jon Alexander and happy beyond belief.

Irena supposed that, in an indirect way, she had Ryan to thank for her mother's happiness. Wanda Yovich would have never moved to Seattle and wound up being Wanda Alexander if she hadn't told her mother she was never coming back to Hades. Because of Ryan.

Irena leaned her forehead against the window, looking at the desolate land.

Funny how "never" wound up having a finite life span. But she knew in her heart once she received her grandfather's phone call telling her that Ryan Hayes had been found dead by his younger brother, Brody, when he'd come home two nights ago, that she was going back to Hades. There was no way she could stay away.

Ten years ago, after her grandfather's pep talk, she'd come to terms with the fact that she and Ryan would never be married, that the very concept of their marriage would have been a disaster waiting to happen. But she had to admit she felt absolutely awful as she tried to imagine a world without him.

Even now, as she waited for June to finally land the small passenger plane, Irena could feel her eyes beginning to sting once more as the impact of the loss struck her again.

Get angry, idiot. In the end, he treated you like dirt. You know that. He's not worth your tears.

But it wasn't in her to be angry—not anymore. Time

and distance had allowed her to view the past in a calmer frame of mind. She wasn't that heartbroken eighteen-year-old. She was twenty-eight and, having dealt with a larger cross-section of humanity in Seattle than she ever could have if she'd remained in Hades, she viewed things differently now. She could see why Ryan had been the way he had, at least in part.

When it came to the reasons for Ryan's wanton, misguided behavior, there was an incredible amount of blame to lay at more than just one doorstep. For starters, nothing was expected of him. Born to wealth, he had none of the pressures that the average person in Hades was faced with. Ryan didn't have to hustle, didn't have to try to help support his family, or even himself for that matter. Life didn't present him with any challenges, other than seeing just how many women he could bed.

In addition, he had no immediate role models to turn to. Certainly not his father. Eric Hayes had moved to Alaska, specifically to Hades, with his two young sons when he'd lost his wife in a freak boating accident. At the time, Hades was as far away from humanity as he could go without literally moving into a cave.

Some people said that the reason for his downward spiral was because he couldn't live with the guilt of knowing that he might have been able to save his wife from a watery grave but had been too involved in saving himself to notice that she had fallen overboard, as well. The only way Eric could find to get even temporary respite from the inner pain was to anesthetize himself with alcohol. As time passed, it took more and more to achieve numbness.

He passed that lesson on to his older son. Ryan had once boasted to her that he'd had his first drink, served to him by his father, when he was nine. At the time, not wanting to be judgmental, she'd told herself that it was just Ryan's way. That he could walk away from drinking any time he wanted to. The problem was that he didn't want to.

But she was so blindly in love with him, so certain that he loved her back until that fateful evening. In the months that followed, she'd often wondered if Ryan wanted her to discover him with Trisha. He knew her penchant for turning up early. Did he thrive on the wild rush of getting away with it, or had he wanted to show her that he wanted to move on? He had to have known that finding him like that would devastate her. And he had still done it.

He'd been a piece of work, all right, Irena thought now, trying desperately to shut away the memories. A piece of work and she was an absolute fool for having loved him as much as she had.

And for still having feelings for him.

"Wait until you see Hades." June suddenly spoke up, trying to fill the silence that seemed louder than the plane's small engine.

June anticipated Irena's reaction to the town she hadn't seen in the last ten years as she began the plane's slow descent.

The airstrip where their small fleet of passenger planes were housed was just up ahead. June smiled to herself. Hades really was growing, she thought fondly. And more than just a little. She and Kevin had slowly built up their business. They now had their own air taxi service as well as her original auto repair store. Kevin had encouraged her to buy it back shortly after the wedding. It was as if he'd sensed what it really meant to her. Which was why she loved him so much. He understood her.

"You won't recognize the place."

Irena laughed shortly. "That's good, because I didn't care for the old Hades."

It was a sentiment shared by a great many of the young people in the area. The moment they turned eighteen, many left to find a life less desolate, or, as in the case of Hades, wasn't isolated from the rest of the world for six months of the year. They all felt that Alaska was a good place to be from, but definitely not to live.

"Oh, it wasn't so bad," June told her. She herself had never experienced that urge to flee the way so many, including her older sister, April, had. "But it's really been growing these last ten years. Ike's turned into a real entrepreneur. He and Jean Luc have really helped build up the place."

"Ike?" Irena echoed in surprise. "The guy who runs the Salty Dog Saloon?"

"The very same one," June told her. There was no missing the pride in her voice. "He's gotten things really moving around here. We've got a hotel now, and just last year, Ike and Jean Luc brought a movie complex to Hades. And they've expanded the general store. You wouldn't recognize it."

Irena laughed, shaking her head. June's verbal list of

changes fell woefully short of progress in her book. "Wow, that puts the town into what, the middle of the twentieth century? Only sixty more years to catch up, I guess."

June spared her one glance before focusing back on the runway up ahead.

"Nothing that a good mall and a good lawyer can't fix," she told her friend. "You know, we still don't have a really good lawyer in Hades. We would if you came back." Her teasing tone vanished as she suddenly braced herself. "Hang on, Irena. This last patch can be a little rough."

Irena was about to tell her there wasn't enough money in the world to tempt her to make her return permanent. That she was more than satisfied practicing law in Seattle. Granted, she was only one of a large group of lawyers, but that was just fine. She didn't need the pressure of being the only defense lawyer in a hundred-mile radius. The pace in Seattle was hectic, but still far more to her liking than life in Hades had ever been.

For the moment, she was too busy holding her breath and gripping the armrests to say any of that. The somewhat choppy flight ended with an even choppier landing. Irena continued clutching the armrests until the plane stopped moving. When it finally came to a halt, she realized that her legs felt rubbery. Getting out of the plane was going to be tricky.

June unbuckled her seat belt and turned around, smiling broadly and obviously pleased with herself.

"Got your money's worth that time," she declared. "The landing turned out better than I thought."

"Right," Irena murmured, more to herself than to June. "We could have crashed."

"You're a lot less optimistic than I remember you," June said, only half kidding.

The next moment, a tall, handsome man with just a smattering of gray at his temples had thrown open the small plane's door. His attention was directed to June and not the plane's single passenger.

"That's it, June," he told her firmly. "No more flying for you until the baby's here."

"Honey, you're not showing your best side," June chided.

"That's because my 'best side' had a heart attack, watching you land the plane," he informed her, helping her down.

On the ground, June turned and watched Kevin help her friend down. She smiled beatifically, as if to erase the dialogue that had just transpired.

"Irena, I want you to meet my husband, Kevin. And he doesn't always frown like this."

"Only when June's determined to give me a heart attack," Kevin explained, setting the plane's lone passenger down on the ground beside his wife. Kevin extended his hand to her. "I'm Kevin Quintano."

Irena nodded, thinking that he had kind eyes. She took his hand and shook it. "Irena Yovich."

"Yovich," Kevin repeated. Surprised, he glanced at June before asking, "Any relation to Yuri Yovich?"

About to pick up her suitcase, she watched Kevin take it for her. "He's my grandfather."

The three of them walked to the small terminal that

mostly housed his office and the tools that June used to work on the planes.

"I guess that makes us kind of related," Kevin speculated, "Since Yuri married June's grandmother, Ursula."

Work, as well as a desire not to run into Ryan, had kept her from the wedding; but she'd had her grandfather and his new wife to her home, where she'd held a reception for them that included her mother and her stepfather. "Ursula isn't still the postmistress, is she?"

"Of course she is," June assured her. "The only way my grandmother would ever stop being Hades's postmistress is when they carry her out of the office, feet first."

Irena nodded. Ursula had been the postmistress in Hades for as long as she could remember. "Things really haven't changed all that much," she concluded.

"You'd be surprised," June contradicted. They stopped before the terminal. "Look, if you haven't got a place to stay, I'd love to put you up at our place."

Irena smiled as she shook her head. "Thanks, but my grandfather said he'd never forgive me if I didn't stay with him and his 'bride.'"

June nodded. She knew that her step-grandfather meant it. A sense of family was very important for survival out here.

"They're very cute together," she confided. "And," June added happily, "best of all, he's not showing any sign of wearing out."

"Wearing out?" Irena echoed, not following June's meaning.

"My grandmother buried three husbands," June reminded her. "She's a very vibrant lady for someone in her late seventies."

"Vibrant," Kevin echoed with an amused grin. "I think the word that June is looking for is 'lusty.'"

Irena thought about the colorful postmistress who was also the keeper of the town's gossip. Apparently, just as she thought, despite the new coats of paint that had been applied here and there, not all that much had really changed here.

Chapter Two

Because the wind had started to pick up, Irena waited until they reached the shelter of the small terminal before she asked June, "Is there any place that I can rent a car?"

Because the Hades she knew didn't have the simplest of amenities, she wouldn't have even asked about a car rental agency. But since June had insisted that the small hamlet was well on its way to being a thriving city, she had nothing to lose by asking. Adequate transportation was supposed to be part of a growing city, wasn't it?

"To rent? No," June replied before Irena could even nod her head in response to the question. "But to borrow? Sure."

June spared her husband a glance and Kevin nodded. They had their own form of communication, Irena thought with just a touch of longing.

"Do you remember how to handle a four-wheel drive vehicle?" her friend asked. Again, before she could answer, June was talking again, "Or has city life made you soft?"

"It's like riding a bike," Irena said with a shade more confidence than she actually felt. Challenges always did that to her—made her step up and agree to things she normally would have thought twice about. But in this case, it was all right. Though she'd relied predominantly on public transportation and taxis in the last ten years, she was certain driving anything would come back to her. That was why she'd maintained her driver's license. "You never quite forget how."

June nodded, obviously pleased. Digging into the pocket of her jacket, she produced a set of keys and held them out to her. "You can borrow my car while you're here."

Irena made no attempt to reach for the keys. "I can't do that," she protested.

"Sure you can." To prove it, June placed the keys into Irena's hand and then closed her fingers over them with her own. She pushed Irena's hand back to her. "I insist."

Irena looked down at the keys, torn. She didn't want to be dependent on someone else to get around while she was here, but at the same time, she couldn't just take June's car from her.

"But don't you need a car to get around?"

June nodded toward Kevin. "I'll just steal Kevin's

car. That's the best part of having your husband work with you." June slanted a glance at Kevin's profile and then smiled, her eyes dancing in response to the thought that had just crossed her mind. "Well, maybe not the *best* part, but it's up there."

The June of ten years ago hadn't wanted all that much to do with the male population. She seemed far more outgoing now, reminding her a bit of Ursula, Irena thought.

"Are you sure you want to part with your car?" Irena asked once again.

June waved away her concern. "Don't give it another thought." She cocked her head. "Still remember your way around here?"

The town was spread out, but even so, there wasn't all that much to Hades. A few streets in the center and most of the homes were along the outskirts of town or a bit further out.

"Some things you never forget. I'm going to surprise my grandfather," she explained. "I wasn't sure when I would get here. I think he's expecting me to arrive late tonight."

June nodded, then began to go toward where the vehicles were housed. With summer over, it was time to shelter the cars from critically dropping temperatures. "Let me show you your way around Clarisse."

"Clarisse?" Irena asked, and then she laughed, remembering. "I forgot that you name cars."

"Makes them easier to handle," June replied as if it was the most natural thing in the world to address four-wheeled vehicles by regular names.

* * *

Irena had every intention of driving June's Jeep straight to the cabin where her grandfather lived with his wife. She wasn't completely sure just how she wound up going in the opposite direction. Most likely, nostalgia had directed her, she decided. Before she was fully conscious of her crimes, she headed toward the building where she had spent her early childhood. Before tragedy had found her family.

She remembered the house with warmth. She and her mother had lived there until her father had been killed in the cave-in. Her mother had never sold the house, most likely for the same reason that she found herself driving toward it now. Sentimental attachment.

Part of Irena couldn't help wondering if the building was still standing.

It was.

The feeling of nostalgia grew more intense the closer she came to the house. Accustomed to the bustle of Seattle, Irena thought the old house looked exceptionally lonely.

Maybe she could even stay here until the funeral. At least here she wouldn't feel as if she was in anyone's way or disrupting anyone's daily routine.

Moreover, she wouldn't be forced to put on a public face to mask the emotional turmoil going on inside of her. She wanted time to deal with that on her own, without receiving any well meaning advice from anyone.

Her grandfather would most likely give her an argument about staying here alone, but she could be as stubborn as he was. Something, she knew, that secretly delighted him. And, in the end, he'd bluster but he would agree—and even boast about it to his friends, saying how she was "just like" him.

A movement on the side of the house caught her eye. Irena peered closer.

Her hands tightened on the steering wheel the second she saw him. Her fingers turned icy, brittle, threatening to break off one by one.

Was that…?

It couldn't be.

Oh, God. Ryan?

Her heart pounding, Irena floored the accelerator. The Jeep seemed to jump ahead. In less than a heartbeat, she was all but on top of him.

Standing near the top of a ladder leaning against the house, the man who had caused her heart to stop was patching a hole just underneath the second floor bedroom window.

Her parents' bedroom, she recalled.

Rather than just use wood to haphazardly board the hole up, he employed some kind of compound and applied it carefully to the gaping hole.

She was hallucinating.

She had to be, Irena silently insisted, unable to breathe. She was here for Ryan's funeral. How could he be standing on a ladder, working so diligently when he was supposed to be dead?

Was it all a hoax?

Or had she crashed in June's plane and this was really the afterlife?

If the afterlife was taking place in Hades, it left a good many things to be desired, she thought.

Was she hallucinating?

Getting out of the car, she left the door hanging open and cautiously approached the ladder.

"Ryan?" she whispered uncertainly.

The moment he turned around to look down at her, she saw her mistake. It wasn't Ryan; it was Brody, Ryan's younger brother.

The last ten years had made the brothers look almost eerily alike. Or rather, Brody now looked the way Ryan had then. He had the same body type, the same jet-black hair. The same green eyes, she realized, stilling the quiver in her stomach as he glared down at her.

"No," the deep voice told her, a trace of disappointment in his face. "I'm—"

"Brody," she supplied. "Yes, I know. I'm sorry, but you just looked so much like him…"

"So people tell me." She couldn't tell from his tone if it bothered him or if, being Brody, he just took it in stride.

Brody made his way down the ladder, placing the materials he'd been working with aside when he reached bottom. A lifetime of self-discipline had him banking down the burst of emotion he'd felt upon suddenly seeing her after all this time.

It didn't seem possible, but Irena was even more beautiful than she had been ten years ago. She took his very breath away. Brody paused a moment to collect himself.

"Hello, Irena. How've you been?"

Brody sounded as if they'd seen each other only last month rather than ten years ago. It reinforced her feelings that, despite a few cosmetic things being done, things never changed in Hades.

"Fine. Terrific." Unless Brody'd gotten married, losing Ryan made him the last of his family. Her heart went out to him. And then, because she'd always felt close to Ryan's brother, was always able to talk to him, Irena asked, "Got a hug for an old friend?"

"Always." Opening up his arms, he enfolded her in them.

Inwardly, he braced himself. Brody refused to recognize or even admit to the potpourri of emotions and sensations racing through him. And if the scent of Irena's golden blond hair against his cheek stirred up old memories, he did his very best to ignore them.

For a moment, Irena allowed herself to get swept away. With very little effort, she could almost imagine herself in Ryan's arms. But pretending Brody was Ryan, even for a moment, wasn't going to lead to anything except deeper heartache.

Placing her hands against his chest, Irena created a wedge between them and drew back. She glanced at her old home, then at him. This was the last place she'd expect to find Brody.

"What are you doing here?" she asked.

Squatting down, he deposited his tools back into the case he'd brought. "I never left Hades."

"No." She waved her hand toward the house. "I mean here, at my parents' old home."

Rising, he glanced over his shoulder as if to make sure he understood her meaning. But he was really avoiding eye contact until he got himself completely under control again. Brody hadn't expected that seeing her would have such an effect on him, but it did.

"Getting it ready for you," he answered simply.

Irena looked at him, confused. "You knew I was coming?"

There was a smile in his green eyes. "Your grandfather's married to Ursula."

Well, that certainly answered the question. If Ursula knew, everyone knew.

"I forgot about that." And then Irena backtracked. "But if you know that, then you'd also have to know that I'm supposed to be staying with my grandfather and Ursula while I'm in Hades."

"I do," he acknowledged. "I also remember how independent you liked to be. I figured there was a good chance that you'd want to be on your own, at least part of the time."

Irena smiled at him. If only his brother had been half as intuitive, half as dependable as Brody, life might have turned out very differently for her and Ryan. "You always did know me so well."

"Yeah, I did, didn't I?"

Didn't help me, though, did it, Irena? Brody couldn't help thinking, although his expression never changed. He'd learned long ago how to mask his feelings so that no one ever suspected how in love he'd been with his brother's girl.

"If you do want to stay here," he went on, "I've had the electricity turned on. And the water. The telephone is going to take me a little longer to get up and running so you might want to use Yuri's line if you need to make a call to anyone, let them know you've arrived safely, things like that."

There was no one to call. Her mother and stepfather were away on a cruise, and she didn't keep in close contact with anyone else. Her boss, Eli Farley, certainly didn't need to be notified of her safe arrival.

Her hand in her pocket, Irena curled her fingers around her cell phone. Taking it out, she held it up. "I take it there's still no cell phone reception."

He surprised her when he didn't automatically confirm her assumptions. "There's some, actually. But it plays by its own set of rules. Reception has a tendency of whimsically going in and out."

Irena laughed. "Not all that different from the lower forty-eight."

She saw the corners of his mouth curve. Unlike Ryan, Brody's smile was boyish—or at least it had been, she realized. There was something almost sexy about it now. Or was that just her imagination, running off with her like it had when she'd first glimpsed Brody and thought he was Ryan?

"What?" she asked, wanting to be let in on the joke if there was one.

"Nothing, you just sound like a tourist instead of a native."

"I'm not a native anymore," she told him. "My home is in Seattle these days. I just came…" Suddenly, her voice failed her. For a second, emotion choked her throat, blocking her words. This was silly, she silently insisted. Fighting past it, she tried again. "I just came—"

"For closure?" Brody supplied.

Closure. My God but that sounded so trendy, so pretentious. She wasn't here for closure; she was here to say goodbye to her youth. To love, because she'd loved Ryan Hayes with all of her young, naive heart. Loved him the way she'd never loved again and in all likelihood, would never love again.

"To pay my respects," she finally concluded.

Brody stared at her for a long moment. "I doubt if you really mean that." He saw the surprise on her face. She opened her mouth to protest. He cut her off. "He was my brother and I loved him, but Ryan didn't deserve anyone's respect. Because he never gave any."

She hadn't expected that from Brody. He'd always been so easygoing. "You've gotten harder than I remember."

"Not harder, just more honest," he corrected. "But I should have been harder. Maybe if someone had gotten tougher with Ryan, if someone took the trouble to shake him up a little and made him fly right, he might still be around."

It wasn't easy keeping the sorrow out of his voice. He still hadn't worked through the anger he felt. Anger because at bottom, he felt what Ryan had done was a waste. It was a terrible, terrible waste of a human life.

Looking back, he supposed it had been a waste for a very long time.

She placed her hand on his arm, feeling his pain. Brody had never been one to talk about his feelings. Maybe they could help one another.

"What happened, Brody?" she asked softly. "My grandfather said that Ryan...that he died by his own hand." It was a polite way of saying that he committed suicide, but she just couldn't bring herself to use the words. It was just too awful to imagine Ryan willingly killing himself.

"That was the immediate cause of death," Brody confirmed. Ryan had been found in a pool of blood, holding the gun that he'd used to end his life. "But the process for Ryan started long before this Monday." He saw the look that came into her eyes and instantly realized what she was thinking. Irena had a tendency to take things on, to shoulder blame where there wasn't any. "No, not ten years ago. You're not to blame," he said firmly. "Hell, you were the best thing that ever happened to him, but he was too dumb at the time to realize it. And as for what I just said, Ryan started destroying himself long before you left."

Guilt still spouted, taking root at the speed of light. If she'd remained, maybe she could have helped Ryan, kept him from destroying himself.

"But if I hadn't left—"

Brody shook his head. In his own way, when it came to Irena and Ryan, it was Ryan who had the strong personality. He could always bend Irena to his will.

"If you hadn't left, Ryan would have probably managed somehow to take you down with him." A hint of a smile surfaced again. "Although I don't know. You were always pretty strong."

She laughed at the notion, shaking her head. "I certainly didn't feel strong."

"Well, you were," he contradicted. "Nobody else ever walked out on Ryan. When you did, it really shook him up. I thought—hoped—that it would wind up being a wake-up call for him. Instead, he just wound up drinking a little more."

She knew it wasn't his intention, but the words cut deep. "Then it *was* my fault."

"No," he insisted. *Damn you, Ryan, you're dead and you're still messing with her.* "It wasn't your fault any more than it was my fault." He took her hands in his as he spoke. "Don't go down that path, Irena. It's self-destructive, and there's nothing to be gained. Ryan was a big boy and he *was* responsible for himself. He had looks, money, charm. He could have done anything, but he wanted to be a drunk." Brody's mouth twisted in a cynical smile. "Not the wisest of career choices. My father certainly proved that. His death should have served as a warning to Ryan. But it didn't."

Her eyes searched his face. "How did you manage to escape?"

Brody shrugged. It was a question that he'd asked himself more than once in the last decade, whenever a sadness gripped him or when his spirits plummeted so low he couldn't even locate them.

"I supposed what saved me was that I wanted to be everything that they weren't. Instead of focusing on me, I looked around and saw that I could be accomplishing things with my life, with my money, beyond just making Ike a wealthy man." He grinned. "No offense to Ike."

She didn't quite follow him. "Ike? How does he figure into it?"

"Ike and his cousin, Jean Luc, own the Salty Dog, the saloon that Ryan practically lived in during the last few years of his life. Whenever he was there, Ike would cut him off at a sensible point or refuse to allow him to be served if Ryan came in already a couple sheets to the wind. But—I don't know if you heard—Ike and his cousin have a number of irons in the fire these days, and he divides his time between different establishments when he's not home, doting on his wife and kids. I couldn't expect him to be Ryan's guardian angel."

"I heard about the first part," she told him, "but not the second. Ike's married?" It seemed impossible to imagine. Almost as impossible as imagining Ryan married, but for a different reason. Ike was, or had been, a flirt, but he'd made no secret of the fact that he loved women and felt that each had a unique quality all her own. "Ike, the eternal bachelor?"

Brody grinned again. "Not anymore. His sister, Juneau, died, leaving her baby daughter for him to raise. He got really domestic after that. And when Dr. Shayne Kerrigan's wife had her best friend come up for a visit, Ike just lost his heart."

Pausing in his narrative, Brody looked up at the sky. It was swiftly turning an ominous shade of gray, and once again, the wind was picking up.

"You know, I don't mind catching you up this way, but I think that we should either do it inside the house, or better yet, drive over to your grandfather's before it snows and strands us here."

Although, he added silently, that wouldn't exactly be the worst thing in the world. How often had he played that very scenario in his head—he and Irena, stranded in a cabin? And it had always ended the same way, with Irena suddenly realizing that she'd loved him all along and not Ryan.

"I know that Yuri's anxious to see you again—and he'll worry until he sees you walk through the door, especially if it starts snowing again."

"Maybe you're right," she agreed.

"I always am." There was a twinkle in his eye as he appraised her.

Irena laughed, feeling the tension drain away. Brody could always make her relax, she thought. She'd missed him. Missed talking to him. She'd shared a good part of her childhood with him, and all of her feelings. It felt good, finding out that she could pick up almost where she'd left off with him.

"God, it's good to see you," she told him with feeling.

She couldn't quite fathom the smile that played across his lips. "Right back at you."

Moved by impulse and fueled by a swirling mixture of feelings that she had yet to label, Irena threw her arms around Brody and kissed him. She kissed him for a number of reasons. To connect to the past, to show Brody her gratitude that the years hadn't changed him. And maybe just because she needed to.

She hadn't expected him to pull back.

Chapter Three

"I'm—I'm sorry," she stammered. "I didn't mean to…"

Embarrassed, at a loss as to what to say, Irena felt color creeping up her neck to her cheeks. She abruptly turned away and was about to hurry into her vehicle.

But Brody caught her by the arm, preventing her getaway. "Sorry," he said, apologizing for his reaction. "You just caught me off guard, that's all."

After years of reining in his feelings whenever he was around her, he'd reacted instinctively and pulled back.

But there was no reason to react that way anymore. Irena was no longer Ryan's girl, not even if his brother were still alive. More so now that Ryan was gone. He didn't have to keep her at a respectful arm's length or secretly enjoying the contact between them while behaving as if she were his sister instead of the woman he'd been in love with since middle school. He was free to make his feelings known—if he so chose.

Old habits died hard.

"No, it's my fault," Irena said, not wanting him to feel as if he had done anything wrong. The misstep was hers. "For a second, it was as if no time had gone by at all." Color flushed over her cheeks again as she told him, "I just took it for granted that you were still just Brody."

Smiling Brody assured her, "I am."

"I mean—"

Since when had her tongue gotten so thick and unwieldy? Finding the right words had never been a problem for her. These days, she stood up in front of juries, making brilliant summations. That wasn't her observation; it belonged to Eli Farley, the oldest senior partner of the firm. And very little pleased Eli, not the least of which was her taking time off to fly to Hades. She'd made sure that her cases were all well covered. Eli had still been displeased.

But, despite her ability to find the right word at the right time, her mind was close to a blank right now. Why was that?

Because she'd made a mistake, taken a situation for granted, and she shouldn't have.

"You're probably happily married and here I am, behaving as if we were still in high school. If your wife saw us—"

"There is no wife," he told her quietly, cutting into her words. "I'm not married."

Irena closed her mouth and looked at him. Brody was such a wonderful person. Why hadn't some woman snatched him up by now?

"You're not? Why?"

Brody glanced down at her left hand and saw that it was conspicuously devoid of jewelry. "Why aren't you married?" he countered.

She shook her head, not about to focus on herself. "I asked first."

"I've been too busy working to take time out to cultivate the kind of relationship women out here have come to expect." *And because the only woman I ever loved left ten years ago.*

He'd come to realize falling in love was not an inalienable right guaranteed to happen. Love was a mysterious emotion made up of many components. He'd never had all the pieces available to him once Irena *had* left Hades.

"Busy?" she repeated, her curiosity aroused. "Doing what?" Ryan had told her that his father had left them both enough money to make sure that neither one of them ever needed to work. And Ryan, she knew, had taken full advantage of that.

But then, Brody had always been different from his brother. Now that she thought about it, the fact that he had dedicated himself to a career didn't really surprise her.

"Using the funds that Dad left us to help out some of the less fortunate people in the area."

He should have known that it wasn't enough to satisfy her. Instead, it only raised more questions.

"Less fortunate?" she repeated, raising her voice to

be heard above the wind that had begun to moan. "And how do you help them?"

He didn't want to talk about himself. Because the temperature was dropping, Brody raised her collar for her. Tiny fingers of emotion swept all through him as he did so. He caught himself just drinking in the sight of her. Before he knew it, she'd be gone again. Leaving the same void she'd left the first time.

He nodded toward the house. "Do you want to go inside?"

That was why she had come here first, Irena reminded herself. The sight of Brody, looking so much like his brother, had driven that right out of her head. But now she nodded.

"Sure."

The front door was unlocked. Pushing it open, she walked in. Irena fully expected to find a mess. After all, time had a way of taking its toll, and neither she nor her mother had lived here for more than eighteen years. They'd moved out when Yuri insisted they come live with him shortly after his son had been killed during the cave-in.

Hesitating at first, her mother had wound up agreeing because she just couldn't bear to stay in a house haunted with memories. Memories that lived in every corner of the single-story house and would ambush her without any warning.

But, by the same token, because there were so many memories here, her mother couldn't bring herself to part with the house and sell it. So it had remained in the family. A silent shadow of the past.

Irena scanned the rooms. Instead of being buried under the grit of almost two decades, the house was amazingly spotless. There wasn't so much as a spider's web visible anywhere.

Stunned, she turned to Brody. He'd mentioned electricity and water and she'd seen him making repairs. Had he cleaned up the rooms as well?

"Did you—"

Brody knew what she was going to ask. "No, can't take the credit for this," he told her. "Sydney, Marta, Alison, Lily and some of the other women from town pitched in to clean this up, just in case you wanted to stay here."

He didn't add that it had been his initial suggestion to Dr. Shayne Kerrigan's wife that had gotten the ball rolling. Remembering how she had felt when she had first come to Hades and had seen the chaotic condition of Shayne's house, Sydney had instantly gotten her friends together to restore order in the abandoned residence.

Irena eyed him, puzzled. "I don't know any of them." Why would total strangers do something like this for her?

Again, he could see the unspoken question in her eyes. Ten years and he could read her like a book. He didn't know if that was a good thing or a bad thing.

"Did you forget how neighborly everyone is here?" he asked her.

She had a nodding acquaintance with her neighbors back in Seattle, but for the most part, she didn't even know their names and they didn't know hers. Anonymity was something she had come to take for granted.

"I suppose I did." Her eyes swept over the living room again, remembering happy times. She didn't realize that she was smiling now. "This is wonderful. You've got to introduce me to Sydney and the others so I can thank them properly."

He'd forgotten how much he enjoyed just watching her react to things. He'd loved her innocence, her naïveté back then. There was still a glimmer of the girl she used to be in the woman she had become. The discovery warmed him. "No problem. You'll probably meet them at the Salty Dog tonight."

"Excuse me?" She had no real firm plans, other than seeing her grandfather and going to the funeral parlor where Ryan was laid out.

"Another thing you forgot," Brody observed, amused. "The people here like to throw parties to welcome people when they come to Hades," he told her, watching her face for any signs that she remembered what he was talking about.

She recalled the tradition, but it didn't apply to her. "But I'm not staying long," she reminded him.

"Doesn't matter. There's still going to be a party. Lily's been cooking all day." The look on her face told him she needed another clarification. "Lily runs the main restaurant here."

"Ike's got competition?" As she recalled, the Salty Dog Saloon offered simple meals to its patrons, which virtually included the entire population of Hades.

"He couldn't begin to compete with Lily's," Brody told her. "The restaurant Lily ran in Seattle won awards."

"Then what's she doing here?"

"Being in love," Brody told her simply. "Lily married Max, the sheriff."

"Oh, right, April told me that," she recalled.

Brody looked down at her hand again. "Okay, I told you why I'm not married." And, since he was baring his soul, he had the right to ask her a question. "Now it's your turn. Why are you still single?"

Irena shrugged, pretending to look around the house some more. She really didn't like talking about herself. They had that in common, she recalled. "Same reason."

"Too busy helping the less fortunate?" he guessed, tongue in cheek.

Irena laughed. This time, she looked at him. "No, wise guy, too busy with work to take the time to socialize."

That was only part of it. He still had the ability to know when she was lying. "Oh, I thought maybe it had something to do with the way Ryan thoughtlessly broke your heart."

She shrugged again, uncomfortable with the way Brody had honed in on the reason. She wasn't used to blatant honesty anymore. It pleased her that Brody could still see through her smoke screen and lies.

"There was some of that, too," she admitted. Then, because they verged on an uncomfortable topic, she turned the conversation back to him. "So, what is it that you do to 'help the less fortunate,' exactly?"

He saw through her but knew when not to push. Irena could get extremely stubborn if she was pushed.

"Whatever it takes." He smiled as he thought about what he had managed to organize. "There's an impressive network here in Hades. Sydney and Marta volunteer some of their free time to help teach some of the Native American children who have fallen behind, get their grades up to par. Dr. Shayne, his brother Ben and Dr. Jimmy, April's husband, as well as Alyson, who's a nurse-practitioner at the clinic—and Jimmy's sister—" he added as a sidebar, trying to educate her about the dynamics in Hades as he went along "—volunteer some of their so-called free time to help treat the families on the reservation. I reimburse them for the medicines as much as I'm able."

He was being modest, as always. Brody always did play down his part in things, but she knew better. She had no doubt that he was the mover and the shaker behind all this, knew that while the others might have had good intentions, it was Brody who had organized them and turned them into a well-oiled machine.

How different Brody was from his late brother. Ryan had wanted nothing more from life than to have a good time. That involved women and alcohol and a great deal of indulgence. Brody's idea of a good time was helping others.

"You should take some time for yourself," she urged when he finished telling her about the program he had going.

"I get a lot of pleasure doing what I do, knowing that in some small way, because of me a kid didn't have to go to bed hungry tonight. Knowing that because I hooked him up to Shayne or Jimmy or Ben, another sick kid will get the treatment he needs in order to get well."

Her eyes crinkled as she smiled at him. "Very noble, Brody."

But he shook his head. "Not noble, just right," he corrected.

Irena stopped wandering around the immaculate house and turned to look at him. He had sounded so somber just now. As if he was on some kind of a solemn mission. She could only think of one thing that would make him feel like that. "Are you trying to make up for your brother and father?"

That would take two lifetimes, Brody thought. At least. Most likely, more.

He shook his head. "Just trying to do my fair share, that's all." He debated saying the next words, then decided that he had nothing to lose. "If you want, the next time I go to the Kenaitze village, you're welcome to come with me."

"I'd like that," she said, then felt she needed to qualify her answer. "If I'm still here."

He inclined his head. "That was understood." It was getting dark within the house. He started to cross to the nearest light switch on the wall, then stopped. He looked at Irena over his shoulder. There was a big, gray flagstone fireplace in the living room. "I can light a fire in the fireplace if you'd like," he offered.

She glanced at the fireplace. Her father had toasted marshmallows with her there one year. Marshmallows had never tasted so good.

"It sounds wonderfully cozy," she acknowledged.

He picked up the note of slight hesitation in her voice and interpreted it. "But you really need to get going."

So far, he'd guessed everything right. It didn't surprise her. Her smile began in her eyes. "Still clairvoyant, I see."

"Just with certain people." Actually, the only one he seemed to be in sync with was her, but he refrained from mentioning that. He didn't want her getting the wrong idea. Or, in this case, the right one.

"Am I that transparent?" she asked. Her laugh rang a little flat to her ears.

Brody was quick to reassure her. "I just know how you think. Nice to know that some things haven't changed."

"I don't imagine too much has changed here." Despite what June had told her, she added silently. How much growth could there have been? Their population had only increased by twenty or so, according to the atlas she'd glanced at before leaving for the airport.

"You'd be surprised," he said, turning toward the window that faced the front of the house. Snow began to fall languidly. How soon before that turned into a blizzard? "Tomorrow, weather permitting, I'll take you around town so you can see for yourself."

He made it sound like an all-day undertaking. She knew better. "What will we do with the other twenty-three and three-quarter hours?"

He laughed. "Hades has gotten bigger," he insisted. "Really."

She studied him for a moment, vaguely aware that his features had matured in a way that made him even better looking. "Is that pride I hear in your voice?"

Brody was about to deny it, then stopped to reconsider. "Yeah, I guess maybe it is. Surviving and thriving against the odds is an accomplishment to be proud of."

Something in the way he said it caught her attention. "Are you talking about the town, or yourself?"

"Actually," Brody admitted, "I was thinking about you."

He knew she was right, that they had to get going, but he was in no hurry to leave. Once they were outside, he fully intended to guide Irena to her grandfather's house. It was already getting dark—they were in that half of the year where, very quickly, there would be a minimum of light available to them—and even natives had been known to lose their way in a storm. And, unless he missed his guess, the sky looked as if it was ready to blanket the area with snow.

But once he was in his car and she in hers, they couldn't talk anymore, and he really enjoyed talking to her. He savored it now, especially since he had no idea when the next opportunity might arise. And besides, before he knew it, she'd be gone again.

He leaned his hand against the wall above her head, unconsciously creating a small alcove for them. "We all expected you to come back, you know." Hoped, really, he added silently. "At first, from college and then after you graduated. But you didn't."

She shrugged, looking away. "Things didn't work out that way." And then she looked back up at him. "You went away to college, too," she remembered.

He'd thought that he could forget her if he was busy enough. He was wrong. "Yeah, but I came back."

"You had no reason not to." She remembered that he had been one of the few who had no desire to escape Hades. "You weren't trying to forget something."

"Maybe I was, in my own way."

The moment the words were out, he regretted them. He had no idea what made him say that. He kept his feeling to himself all this time, not saying a word to anyone, although he suspected that Ryan had known.

It wasn't typical of his brother not to bring it up, not to tease him. Sensitivity had never been Ryan's strong suit, but in this one instance, somehow his brother had known enough to leave the subject, his feelings for Irena, alone.

Except for that one time.

It was the day before he took his own life. Ryan had been oddly forthright and talkative that afternoon, going over a litany of the mistakes he'd made over the years. He remembered that Irena had appeared twice on his brother's list. Once because he regretted treating her so badly and the second time because, Ryan had told him, he realized that he, Brody, was the one who actually deserved to have her.

"Irena deserved someone better than me, and you deserved someone like her," Ryan had concluded that day, being unusually serious. "If it hadn't been for me getting in the way, who knows? Maybe the two of you might have gotten married. Or at least had a lot of fun together." Ryan had winked then and chuckled. He'd wound up having a coughing fit.

"You're babbling now," he'd remembered telling his brother, doing his best to get Ryan to bed so that he could sleep it off. Four o'clock in the afternoon and Ryan was already drunk out of his mind.

"Maybe," Ryan had allowed, falling into bed like a child-worn rag doll. "But I'm babbling the truth." Ryan had grabbed the front of his shirt, raising himself off the bed for a moment as he underscored his point. "I know you love her. It's there in your eyes."

He'd very gently disengaged Ryan's fingers from his shirt and put him back down again. "You're hallucinating, Ryan," he'd said with feeling.

"No, I'm not," Ryan insisted. "I've always known it. Maybe that was even the reason I went after her," he'd admitted, not because he was proud of himself, but because, Brody now realized, his brother had needed to confess the deed. "Because I wanted to take what you wanted. I'm sorry, Brody, I'm sorry." He began to cry then. "I screwed up for all of us."

It had taken him a while to calm Ryan down again. As for the apology, at the time he'd chalked up the words as the ramblings of an alcoholic. He'd heard enough so-called confessions and protestations of regret from both his father and his brother to know that there would be no memory of this in the morning.

But instead, this time there was no Ryan in the morning.

It was the last conversation they'd had.

"What?" Irena asked now, pressing him for an answer. "What were you trying to forget?"

Brody shook his head. "Sorry, didn't mean to come off sounding so melodramatic." He glanced out the front window again. It was looking worse by the minute.

"If we don't leave now, we're going to wind up getting snowed in here," he warned again. "Without any working phone lines, we'll be stranded."

"My grandfather would find us," she assured him with a fond smile. "He has this uncanny instinct when it comes to family. But," she agreed, lifting up the hood of her parka, "there's no reason to put it to the test. You're right, let's go."

Brody closed the door behind him as he followed her out. He didn't bother locking it. Everything worth stealing had just walked out ahead of him.

Chapter Four

"You are really being here, Little One! It is so wonderful to be seeing you!"

The moment Yuri Yovich threw open his front door and saw who was standing on his doorstep, joy exploded all over his sun-weathered face. The rugged ex-miner looked at least a full decade younger than his seventy-nine years.

He gleefully swept his granddaughter into a fierce, warm embrace as, momentarily lapsing into Russian, he offered up several words of thanksgiving that she had arrived safely.

Creating a little space between them, he anointed first her left cheek, then her right in a traditional, exuberant greeting.

"I am so sorry that this is not being a happier occasion for you," he confessed, pulling her to him once more. "I did not think you are coming until later. Why for you did not call me?" he asked, his accent thickening in the wake of his excitement at her arrival. "I would have coming to get you."

Looking over her head, Yuri realized that his granddaughter was not alone. One arm around Irena, he motioned Brody in with the other. "Ah, Brody, thank you for bringing her to me." He quickly closed the door to keep out the cold.

Brody smiled as he shook his head. Yuri should know better, he thought, placing her suitcase on the floor. "No one 'brings' Irena, Yuri. She drove herself here. I just followed to make sure she got here safely."

Yuri turned toward Irena, confused. Had she driven from the Anchorage airport? "You are driving? With a car? How is this possible?"

Very few vehicles could make, or even attempt to make, the trip from Anchorage to Hades this time of year. September was the beginning of the six-month period that, before Shayne Kerrigan had bought a plane, the citizens of Hades found themselves completely cut off from the rest of the world.

"June flew me in, and she insisted that I use her Jeep," Irena explained. "I offered to rent it, but she wouldn't hear of it."

Yuri nodded with feeling, his shaggy gray hair swaying. "Ah, now I am understanding. June, she is a good girl." Beaming, he framed Irena's face with his massive hands. "Let me looking at you." Joy vibrated in every word he uttered. "It is being much too long, Little One."

"Yes, it has," she agreed. She'd forgotten how much she loved this bear of a man with his gentle touch and flowing mane. "You and Ursula should come and visit me more often."

"Ahh," he made a little noise as he waved his hand at the suggestion. "I am not liking all that city noise. Better that you are here. How is your mother? Well, I am hoping."

"She's very well," Irena assured him. "And very much in love."

"Love is good," he said with feeling, again nodding his head. The pronouncement led him to think of the larger than life woman he had finally talked into marrying him. Thoughts of Ursula always made him smile. "Ursula will be so happy to be seeing you." And that led him to yet another thought. "Oh," he said as if suddenly startled.

"Oh?" Irena echoed, both amused and curious. Glancing at Brody, she saw him raise his shoulders, letting her know that he had no clue why the older man looked as if he'd just become aware of something.

"I am needing to leave. I must picking up my bride from where she is working." Yuri went to the coatrack and removed his parka. "I am telling her she should stop, but she is refusing." He lowered his voice, as if to share a secret. "She likes being the post person." Shoving his arms into the sleeves of his jacket, he sighed dramatically. But it was obvious that he wasn't really upset about the situation. "Ursula is doing what she is wanting to do." Pulling a colorful scarf out of his pocket, he draped it over his neck. "I will be coming right back," he promised.

Yuri paused to peer out the front window. "The snow, it is stopping. You bring me good luck," he announced, kissing Irena on both cheeks again. And then he turned to Brody. "You will staying to keep her company until I be back?"

She didn't want Brody to be put on the spot. "Grandpa, I don't need a babysitter."

"No babysitter. Friend," Yuri answered innocently. He glanced at Brody for confirmation. "And everyone is needing friend, yes?"

"Yes." She laughed. Irena tucked the ends of her grandfather's scarf into his jacket and then pulled up the zipper for him. "Be careful."

"Always," he said solemnly, kissing her forehead. And then, just as he was about to leave, he tossed off, "And when I coming back, we go."

Surprised, Irena caught his arm to stop him. "Go? Go where?"

Yuri looked at his granddaughter incredulously. "Where we always are going to celebrate. To the Salty Dog."

Brody merely smiled at Yuri's statement as the older man left the house. Once Yuri was gone, Brody looked at Irena. "I told you there'd be a get-together at Ike's."

She appreciated that her grandfather was happy to see her, appreciated that old friends wanted to see her, but the truth of it was, she didn't feel very festive.

"I'd rather go to the funeral parlor," she told Brody.

"There's not much point in you going, especially not tonight." He saw the quizzical look that came into her eyes. "It's a closed casket," he explained. "Nathan and his wife couldn't make Ryan presentable enough for viewing."

He left it at that, not elaborating that Ryan had obviously placed the muzzle of his gun underneath his chin. It was the ultimate irony. Ryan's looks were what his older brother had always traded on. His face had been his free ticket to countless bedrooms, and in the end, he'd destroyed it. Intentionally? There was no way of knowing, but he did have his suspicions.

Irena could feel her heart constricting. She'd forgotten that Ryan had shot himself. Hadn't thought through the repercussions of that act.

Maybe it was better this way. She thought of herself as a trooper, but seeing Ryan laid out in a casket might be more than she could bear.

She nodded in response. "I'd still like to pay my respects."

He didn't want her going by herself. No matter how independent she was, she still needed someone to lean on at a time like this, and who better than a friend? "Tell you what, if you can be ready by eight, I'll take you tomorrow morning."

By her schedule, eight was far from early, but he obviously thought it was, so she asked, "Why so early?"

"I promised Matthew Long Wolf I'd come by the reservation early tomorrow morning."

Not wanting to remain idle, where memories could assault her, she impulsively asked, "Can I come along with you?"

The request caught him off guard. But then he realized that it wasn't that she wanted to be with him; she probably just wanted to see what he was up to. Still, the end result was the same. He'd be around her.

"Sure. Happy to take you." He paused for a moment, studying her. Her hands were soft, her nails manicured. She probably wasn't used to working with them. "How handy are you with a hammer?"

A teasing smile played on her lips. "It all depends on what I'm supposed to be doing with that hammer."

"You'd be pounding in nails."

"Into anything in particular?" Irena asked.

"A house. Or what's hopefully going to be a house by the end of the week."

"Tell me more, Brody, or I might wind up using that hammer more creatively."

He laughed. "You always did have a way with words. No wonder you became a lawyer."

"Talk now, flattery later," she instructed.

"Some of the older houses on the reservation are either on the verge of falling apart or already have. With winter around the corner, we're running out of time. If they don't have proper living facilities, a lot of the people living there risk getting sick. A few years ago, there was a flu epidemic that took more lives than it should have." Because Irena was looking at him, cocking her head first to one side, then the other, he stopped talking about his agenda. "What are you doing?"

The expression on her face was innocence personified. "Just looking for the halo."

He frowned. "Very funny."

When he frowned like that, he looked just like Ryan, she thought. Except that Ryan wouldn't have been caught dead being so selfless.

"No, actually, very admirable," she said seriously. "I'd like to make a contribution to this work of yours." She picked up her purse and took out her checkbook.

Brody placed his hand over hers, aborting her search. "A willing pair of hands is more than enough."

She'd already said she'd help, but she wanted to do more. Should do more since she'd once lived here. "No one can ever have enough money."

"Yeah, they can," he told her. "My father and Ryan had more than enough for the rest of their lives and look where it got them. My father drank himself to death and Ryan 'executed' himself."

A wave of guilt went through her. Irena pressed her lips together. She'd walked right into that, didn't she? "Sorry. I didn't think."

"No, you did. You were thinking of the people on the reservation, and you were being generous. It's not that I don't appreciate the offer, but really, having you pitch in tomorrow is more than enough. Everyone's got more than enough to do here." Life in Hades could be very hard. "Getting volunteers isn't always easy."

She nodded, then her eyes grew bright as she had an idea. "You could call it a party."

Her eyes mesmerized him. It took effort to tear his own away and focus on what she was saying. "What?"

"Well, as you pointed out, the citizens of Hades love getting together for a little celebration for any reason." She grinned. "Move the party out of Ike's place and to the reservation."

He turned her words over in his head. "You know," he said with a grin, "that just might work."

"Sure it will," she encouraged.

They'd have to do it when they had daylight, which meant the heart of the day. But if they had enough people, a lot could be accomplished. He recalled that that was the way the firehouse had been built. "Maybe I'll try it next weekend."

Next weekend. She'd be gone by then. Back to her life. She almost felt sorry. The key word being "almost." "Too bad I won't be here to see how it goes."

Though his expression never changed, Brody felt something inside of him plummet. "How soon do you have to leave?"

She'd purposely left her return ticket open-ended because her grandfather hadn't been certain when the funeral was going to be held. She still didn't know. "I was thinking the day after the funeral. By the way, when is the funeral?"

He had made all the arrangements yesterday afternoon. And after that, he'd gotten on his treadmill and run for ten miles, trying to work his way through his grief and silently cursing Ryan for being so damn selfishly stupid.

"Saturday, at eleven," he told her.

Saturday. That meant she had to stay here five days, counting today. She thought of her boss. Eli had wanted her back before she even left. He wasn't going to be happy that she wasn't going to be in until Monday morning. "Then I'll be leaving on Sunday."

Sunday. Today was Wednesday. That gave him three full days. Three days with her. It didn't seem like nearly enough. But he supposed in comparison to not having any time at all, this would have to do.

He had no idea he was going to ask—until he did. "You really have to leave so soon?"

She nodded. "I've got a lot of cases I'm juggling. It was hard enough getting any time off. My boss isn't a big fan of his people having private lives," she told Brody.

That didn't sound like something the Irena he knew would have put up with.

"Are you happy?" he asked her suddenly. She eyed him quizzically. "This lawyering stuff that you do, does it make you happy?"

She felt herself growing defensive. Of late, she found herself becoming combative much too often. A side effect of always having to be on her toes, always fighting to get the best cases.

"I make a difference," she answered. Did that sound as clichéd to him as it did to her? "And that makes me happy."

He tried to understand. "Defending criminals makes you happy?" His voice was heavy with skepticism.

The lawyer in her rose to the surface. "They're not

criminals until they've been proven guilty," she pointed out.

Her firm represented people in the public eye accused of major crimes. He'd followed her career at length. All it took were a few well-placed questions put to Ursula. The gregarious woman was happy to supply all the details.

"Semantics," he responded.

"No," she countered, "the justice system." She could see that he wasn't convinced. It was important to her that he understand. Important for some reason that he approve.

"Not everyone who's arrested is automatically guilty," she pointed out.

Brody slowly nodded. "True enough." And then he apologized. "I've got no right to question what you do with your life."

Since they were apologizing, she took her turn. "I didn't mean to sound so defensive."

The moment hung between them. Brody glanced down at his clothes. He was wearing the oldest jeans he had and the shirt beneath his jacket was ripped in several places, thanks to an altercation he'd gotten into with a stack of planks before he'd gotten a chance to plane them.

"I'd better go home to change," he told her. And then, because he'd envisioned her countless times in the last ten years, he looked at Irena for a moment longer. Trying to absorb enough to see him through the next ten years. Or so. "I'll see you later at the saloon."

"I guess so," she agreed, "seeing as I don't seem to have a choice in the matter."

He paused just before opening the door. His eyes

met hers. "You always have a choice, Irena," he told her solemnly.

And then he walked out into the cold, leaving her to stare at the closed door, wondering if she'd made a mistake coming back.

"How're you doin' darlin'?" Klondike LeBlanc, known to one and all as Ike, asked her warmly. The moment Irena had entered with Yuri and Ursula, Ike had rounded the bar and made his way over to her. He took both her hands in his as he brushed a quick kiss against her cheek.

A feeling of homecoming swelled inside her before she had a chance to shut it down.

This isn't home anymore, she reminded herself.

Nothing had changed. Not the saloon, not Ike, nor the people who filled the establishment, calling out greetings to her the moment she entered. Oh, some of the residents looked a little older, a little more worn, and there were a few new faces. But for the most part, it was almost as if she'd never left. As if Hades had somehow been frozen in time like some mythical township out of a fairy tale.

"I'm fine, Ike," she told him, "and you look just as handsome as ever." He did, she thought. There was still that same twinkle in his eye every time he called a woman "darlin'."

"That's because married life agrees with him," a petite blonde informed her, slipping in next to Ike. She threaded one arm around Ike's waist and turned her face up to his. "Doesn't it, Ike?"

"Absolutely." He grinned broadly and that was when Irena saw it. Contentment. It radiated from every pore. "Didn't know what I was missing until you came along, darlin'," he told his wife.

"Good answer," Marta LeBlanc approved. Her generous mouth curved. And then, as if suddenly aware that they were far from alone in this crowded saloon, Marta extended her hand to Irena. "Hi, I'm Marta, Ike's wife."

"I kind of figured that out," Irena told her, shaking the woman's hand. "Brody told me that you helped clean up my old home. Thank you."

Marta brushed aside the expression of gratitude. "No thanks necessary. Enjoyed doing it. What are neighbors for?" Her eyes were warm as she asked, "So tell us, how long are you planning to stay?"

That made it sound as if she was going to be staying for more than a heartbeat. "I'm not," Irena replied. "I'm leaving right after the funeral. Sunday," she elaborated.

"Oh, you can't go that fast, darlin'," Ike protested. "It hardly gives us a chance to catch up."

Marta exchanged looks with her husband. "That's too bad. Brody will be disappointed."

Something stirred inside Irena. Curiosity? Had Brody said something to Ike? "Why should he be disappointed?"

Ike didn't answer her question. Instead, he brought up another point. "You know, Marta only came up here for a couple weeks." He looked down at his wife. "That was how long ago, darlin'?"

"In another lifetime," Marta responded. And then she looked back at Irena. "This place grows on you."

"Unless you're born here," Irena contradicted.

"Ike was born here," Marta pointed out. "He's never wanted to leave. He just wants to build Hades up."

"What are we talking about?" April Quintano asked, wedging in between them.

Irena recognized the voice, but was surprised when she looked at the woman who joined them. "April?"

"The very same." The other woman laughed and then she threw her arms around Irena. "June told me she flew you in this afternoon." She drew back to get a good look at Yuri's granddaughter. "God, the last time I saw you, you were all knees and elbows."

"And you were on your way out of Hades," Irena recalled. "Never to darken its snowy doorway again."

"Not just out of Hades but out of Alaska," April corrected.

"And now you live here?" Irena questioned.

April laughed. "The best laid plans of mice and men…"

As she recalled, April had been very vocal about how much she hated Hades. She'd left the moment she was old enough to be on her own. The woman who left bore little resemblance to the contented woman standing before her. "What happened?"

"My grandmother, the little sneak," April said with affection, looking over toward Ursula, "supposedly had a heart attack so I came back to help take care of her. At the same time, Jimmy came up to visit his sister." She shrugged. "One thing led to another and I wound up staying." April held up her left hand, displaying the gold band that symbolized their union. "I've never been happier. Neither, he tells me, has Jimmy." Her eyes crinkled as she smiled again. "Gotta be the air here," she quipped.

"Or they're putting something in the water," Irena speculated dryly.

"Whatever it is, it seems to be working," April responded expansively. "We're growing by leaps and bounds these days. A lot fewer people are leaving and some are coming."

"Speaking of coming, there's Brody," Ike commented, pointing toward the doorway. He raised his arm, waving at the man who had just walked in through the door.

At the mention of her childhood best friend, Irena turned to look in the direction of the front entrance. Because the saloon was so crowded, it took her a few seconds to locate him. When she did, she was struck again by how much Brody resembled his brother, especially at a distance.

An eerie feeling swirled through her like a pint-sized lethal twister.

Chapter Five

As the minutes melted into hours, Irena realized she'd forgotten something else: How gregarious the people who lived in Hades were. And how they thought nothing of asking endless personal questions.

They didn't ask out of self-serving curiosity or to use an explosive tidbit against her—not like in her line of work. Hades inhabitants asked questions because they actually cared about the answers. Because they cared about her.

And while Ursula, aided and abetted by her position as Hades' postmistress, was definitely the undisputed queen of information gathering, the people Irena had once regarded as her neighbors weren't far behind.

If they wanted to know something, they found a way to find out—directly or indirectly.

"Stop," Lily Yearling cried after bearing witness to another flood of inquiries. "Let the poor girl just enjoy being back without being interrogated."

Looking at her across the table where a number of them had planted themselves, Lily, the owner and primary chef of Hades' most popular eating establishment, gave her a sympathetic smile. "I know just what you're going through," the woman told Irena. "When this crowd had that first party in my 'honor—'" she deliberately emphasized the word "—I thought my head would explode before the evening was half over. I'd never come up against so many questions in such a short period of time from such innocent-looking people in my life. I felt like I was being dissected and then put back together again." Lily placed her hand on top of hers and leaned forward, as if to impart some newly uncovered secret. "Try to remember they mean well."

"Dissected," Max echoed, shaking his head. "You're exaggerating, Lily."

Lily regarded her husband and smiled, as if appreciating some secret pleasure. "No, I'm not. People don't do that in Seattle," she pointed out. She and her siblings were all natives of the Washington city.

"That's because they're too busy scratching out a living, running people over who get in their way," her sister, Alison, chimed in. "I should know." She turned toward Irena. "I was going to nursing school and driving a taxi part time for Kevin back in Seattle when I met Jean Luc and he sweet-talked me into coming up here."

"Coming up here was your idea," Jean Luc reminded his wife. "You said you wanted to do something to pay me back for saving you from that mugger."

Alison sniffed. "I was thinking more along the lines of giving you a free tour around Seattle, not coming back here to pose as your wife."

"What?" Completely confused, Irena looked from Jean Luc to Alison, waiting for enlightenment. She was only getting a tiny taste of the whole story, and she hated being left in the dark.

"Long story," Jean Luc told her. Then, because she appeared disappointed, he promised, "I'll save it for the next time we're completely snowed in and bored out of our minds."

"She won't be here then," Brody interjected.

Irena looked at him, surprised by his comment. He sat next to her at the table, and for the most part, he'd been very quiet. He hadn't said more than three sentences all evening. But, talkative or not, she hadn't forgotten he was there, not even for a moment. For reasons she couldn't quite understand, his presence seemed to permeate her.

Jean Luc flashed her an apologetic smile. "Oh, yeah, I'm sorry." Even so, this still wasn't the time to drag out a story the others were well acquainted with. "Some other time, then, when Ike isn't hanging around, ready to narrate or embellish everything I say."

Sitting at the far end of the table, Ike grinned at his more subdued cousin. "I just like adding a little color to your stories. It makes them more lively and, more importantly, keeps people from falling asleep."

Marta leaned forward, patting her husband's hand. "Translation, he can't keep quiet for more than two minutes at a time—and even that's a stretch."

Irena had forgotten how well everyone in Hades seemed to get along. There were no cliques here, no elite hierarchy or strictly enforced chain of command that couldn't be violated under pain of censure. Granted, there was a division of labor and everyone had their assigned place in Hades. Sometimes she'd found the slowed-down pace maddening, but if some kind of an emergency arose, they'd all quickly band together and tackle whatever it was that needed their attention.

She didn't realize she was smiling to herself until she heard, "Penny for your thoughts?"

Brody leaned in so that only she could hear his question.

She still wore the same fragrance, he realized. Some stirring mixture of vanilla and jasmine. Every time he walked in the field behind his house when the jasmine were in bloom, the scent always made him think of her.

Lots of things made him think of her.

"Gotta do better than that if you want to hear them." Irena laughed, turning her head to look at him.

"Oh? What would it take to hear your thoughts?" he asked.

The laughter died in her throat, fading away. Her face was only inches from his. Maybe not even inches, maybe just an inch and a heartbeat away. As for her heart, it had sped up and now seemed to vibrate in all her pulse points.

Everyone else in the overly crowded establishment

swiftly faded into the outer perimeters, along with the din they created. A stillness came in their wake, a stillness that surrounded just the two of them and this isolated, overly warm second in time.

"Is it just me," she murmured, the words all but dribbling from her lips in slow motion, "or is it getting hot in here?"

"It's you," Brody said. "Although maybe the fact that so many bodies are jammed into such a limited amount of space might have something to do with it."

Not all that long ago the entire population of Hades was able to fit into the saloon. That was back when Ike and Jean Luc only worked here, before they bought the Salty Dog, the first of their many business ventures. And despite the fact that under Ike and Jean Luc's ownership, the saloon had expanded to more than twice its original size, there still never seemed to be enough room to accommodate everyone.

That was why, for most gatherings, people took turns coming in while others spent time outside. The majority of gatherings were held in the summer months where the sun hung around for an obscene amount of time.

Damn, but he wanted to kiss her. To frame her face with his hands and touch his lips to hers. To taste her the way he'd longed to all these years. But he'd only make a fool of himself. He was glad they were here and not anywhere private.

Brody got a grip on himself. "You look tired," he said.

"Yeah, I guess I am."

She'd arrived in Hades already tired. Her brief time

MARIE FERRARELLA   69

at the office, followed by the long trip had exhausted her. Even so, she didn't want to see the evening end. Other than attending the funeral, she wouldn't see these people again. And a funeral wasn't the place for visiting, for remembering times that had gone into making up her character as well as creating a warehouse of memories.

Leaning over, she picked up her purse and placed it on the table in front of her. "Well, if I'm supposed to get an early start tomorrow, maybe I should go back to the house."

"Mine, I am hoping," Yuri fairly shouted the words to her. Her grandfather began to rise from the table.

She'd actually been thinking of going to her mother's house. But that, she realized, would be insulting the old man, and the last thing she wanted was to hurt his feelings.

Maybe tomorrow night, she promised herself.

"Yes, but you don't have to leave on my account, Grandpa," she shouted back. "I know the way there," she assured him.

"Nights have a way of turning you around," Shayne chimed in, raising his voice as well.

Why was everyone treating her as if she'd just gotten off the plane in Hades for the first time? "I know," she acknowledged. "I lived here for eighteen years. I'm not exactly a novice."

"No, just out of practice," Brody told her, ingratiating himself to Yuri for taking his side in this. "Don't worry, Yuri. I can take her home. It's on my way anyway."

Yuri lowered himself back into his chair. He beamed his thanks—and approval. "Thank you, I am being grateful."

Irena did what she could to suppress the grin that came to her lips. She'd forgotten how endearing it was to listen to her grandfather employ his own version of the English language.

She'd missed that, too, she realized.

"Glad to do it," Brody assured the older man. He removed Irena's parka from the back of her chair and helped her on with it. She looked at him in mild surprise. "Got everything?"

"If she leaves something behind, I'll hold it for her," Ike volunteered before Irena could answer. "Besides, nobody's going to take anything." And then he winked. "Unless, of course, it's a juicy diary. Then I get dibs on that."

"Sorry to disappoint you," Irena tossed over her shoulder as she waited for Brody to put his fur-lined jacket on. "No 'juicy diary.' I never put anything like that in writing."

"Pity." Ike laughed. Marta jabbed him in the ribs with her elbow, and he pretended to wince.

"Such a good boy," Irena heard Ursula tell the others as Brody escorted her toward the front entrance. "Nothing at all like his brother."

Irena cringed inwardly. She slanted a glance at Brody to see if he'd heard. One look at his face told her that he had.

She turned toward him when they reached the door. Sometimes Ursula talked before her brain was adequately engaged. "I'm really sorry you had to hear that."

"Why?" he asked, curious to hear her reasons. "It's true. I am nothing like Ryan. And Ryan knew it, too. He said as much a couple of times. I'm not sure if he thought it was an insult or not." Brody pulled open the door and waited for her to walk through. "He was always trying to get me to be more like him, to kick back and 'pick the fruits of life.' His words, not mine," he said in emphasis.

She recognized them. Ryan had said the same to her when she'd chastised him for not doing anything with his life. And for lying to her when he'd promised to enroll at her college. He'd told her that he was busy picking the fruits of life and that she should try it sometime.

It was part of the last conversation she ever had with him.

The wind seemed to go right through her the moment she walked out of the saloon. Irena picked up her hood, slipping it on her head. She tightened the ties beneath her chin.

"Why didn't you?" she asked, curious. "According to Ryan, there was certainly enough money for both of you to 'kick back and relax.'"

He couldn't picture himself doing that. Or, more specifically, *not* doing anyway.

"It wasn't me," he answered.

Brody led her over to his vehicle. Like everyone else in the area, he didn't keep his car locked any more than he locked his front door. Trust was the key factor in Hades.

He opened the car door for Irena. "Doing nothing makes me restless," he explained. "Everywhere I look, I see things that need doing." He rounded the back of the vehicle and got in behind the steering wheel, closing his door before he continued. He didn't want to have to compete with the wind. "People who need caring for."

Securing her seat belt, she shifted her body to look at Brody. He's always been like this, she recalled. Why hadn't she ever noticed how noble he was?

"If you feel like that, why didn't you become a doctor?"

Brody laughed shortly as he put the key into the ignition. It took two tries to start the vehicle. It always became temperamental whenever the weather became colder.

"I'm not patient enough or skilled enough to be a doctor, Irena. I am good at drumming up people to come help, pounding nails into wood, simple things like that."

The full moon provided the only illumination besides the vehicle's headlights. Night made the surrounding area appear ever so bleak. Much as Irena hated to admit it, she realized that she would have been hard-pressed to find her way to her grandfather's house. Getting turned around out here at night, especially in the winter, happened far more often than people thought.

"That doesn't sound all that simple to me," she told him loyally. "You give quite a lot of yourself."

Brody shrugged off the comment. Unlike his brother, he'd always been uncomfortable with attention or compliments. He liked doing things behind the scenes, without any fanfare. His satisfaction came from accomplishing what he set out to do, whether it was to put food on someone's table, provide a sick mother with medical attention or help a child realize their full potential. He was, he supposed, a matchmaker of sorts, matching people with other people who could help them. That was his gift, his talent, along with his drive. That was enough.

"We all do what we can," he said quietly.

Which meant, in Brody's case, that he went the extra mile—or ten. Irena thought of the people she worked with. All highly educated, all at the top of their class. A great many of them operating without a heart. Compared to Brody, they were a school of barracudas.

"Not all of us," she told him with feeling.

He glanced in her direction for a moment, before looking back on the road. Was she talking about herself, or someone else? Ten years separated their last meeting from now. What had she been doing those years? Had there been someone special? Was there still?

"Something you want to talk about?" he asked her casually.

She'd been so busy living her life, focusing on her career, she hadn't stopped to evaluate it, to see if it was worth it. She'd just assumed that it was; but now, she wasn't as certain as she once had been.

"Not really."

She looked straight ahead. Unlike her mother's house, her grandfather's was just on the outskirts of town, positioned halfway between the town's buildings and the vast wilderness just beyond.

It was hard seeing anything beyond the headlights, even with the moonlight shining down.

This looked like the heart of midnight. "I'd forgotten how dark it is out here."

"It is that," he agreed. "It's kind of soothing after all that noise in the saloon."

Soothing. That wasn't the way she saw it. The word that came to mind for her was "lonely" or maybe just "empty," but she made no further comment. Instead, she leaned forward in her seat and looked up at the stars that were out in full force tonight.

"They seem brighter up here," she commented, then added, "the stars," in case he didn't know what she was referring to.

"That's because they are." He turned and pulled up before the last house on the way out of Hades. "We're here," he announced.

"So we are. Thank you for bringing me home." She hadn't realized that her grandfather's house was up ahead until they were right in front of it.

"My pleasure." She didn't need to thank him. They were friends. Friends did things for one another. Even if one friend was in love with the other.

Irena began to open the door, then stopped. "And you'll be here tomorrow at eight?"

Brody nodded, watching the way the moonlight seemed to frame her where she sat, as if trying to shield her from the darkness.

"That's what I said."

Something distant and warm stirred within her. She smiled fondly at him. "And I could always take what you said to the bank."

The interior of his car seemed to shrink, shrinking to the point where a tiny bit of space between her and him remained. He could hear her breathing, could almost taste her breath on his lips and his senses filled with the scent of her fragrance.

Whether that scent came from a bottle with a designer label on it or was just the intoxicating scent of her skin, he didn't know. He *did* know that if Irena didn't leave his car in the next couple of seconds, he would lose his battle with temptation. Badly.

Since she didn't make a move, he was forced to. Brody opened the door on his side and got out, then came around the back of the vehicle to her side. Opening her door, he stepped back to allow her plenty of space to get out.

She still managed to brush against him when she emerged.

Their eyes met as she began to tender an apology for bumping against him.

The words froze on her lips.

Irena wasn't sure if it was because Brody reminded her of Ryan and she wanted to connect to the past one last time.

Or because she just needed to make contact with someone, even for a moment.

She didn't know, didn't bother to try to reason it out for herself, or even make some half-hearted attempt to talk herself out of it. Instead, she stepped forward, reached up to capture Brody's face in her hands and, her heart pounding, her breath catching in her throat, Irena kissed him.

Chapter Six

There were times, especially when he was younger, when Brody would let his mind drift, unrestrained, uninhibited.

Specifically, he would fantasize what it would be like to kiss Irena. What it would be like to feel her lips against his and get lost in her scent. Lying in bed, wrapped in the soothing darkness of an Alaskan night, he'd wondered what it would be like to make love with her.

He'd sworn silently, more than once, to any deity who might be eavesdropping on his thoughts, that if he *ever* had the incredible good fortune to find out, he would never trample her feelings, never take her for granted.

The way that Ryan did.

This was far better than he'd imagined.

That she would initiate the kiss captured him completely by surprise, sending adrenaline through his hard, lean body.

Brody didn't attempt to fool himself. He knew exactly why this was happening. It was displacement on Irena's part, nothing more. She wasn't kissing him. She was kissing the memory of his brother, and that was all right with him. He would take this kiss any way it was delivered. And besides, he understood the need for comfort. In an odd way, he was doing a good deed.

Closing his arms around her, Brody deepened the kiss she had begun, allowing oh, so briefly his own feelings to emerge just a little. Just enough so that she wouldn't suddenly become embarrassed at what she'd started.

Damn but it was hard not to lose himself in her. Yuri and Ursula were still at the Salty Dog Saloon and probably would remain so for the next hour or more. They would be alone in the house.

Alone together.

And he could…he could…

No, he couldn't, a voice in his head declared firmly. He couldn't, and he knew it, because then he would be taking advantage of Irena's grief, of her vulnerability. And in the process, he would lose her as a friend, something he didn't want to have happen at any cost.

Even if she was only going to be in his life a few more precious days, he couldn't take a chance on sacrificing them, on sacrificing the relationship they had, to satisfy the urgency he felt drumming throughout his body.

So, with effort, struggling more with himself than he ever had before, Brody placed his hands on Irena's shoulders and very gently, but firmly, created a space between them. Then he drew his mouth away from hers, even though everything within him protested loudly.

As he separated himself from Irena, Brody saw the slightly dazed, confused look on her face, the dewy-softness of her eyes as well as the flush of her cheeks. Her expression very nearly made him give in to the demands pounding through his soul. Only the consequences prevented him from following through on his desires.

"It's cold out here," he told her softly, forcing a smile to his lips. "You'd better go inside."

Cold? Was it cold? All she felt was this wild heat flaring all through her. She could have sworn she was close to burning up. Was that the result of misplaced attraction? Or was it embarrassment that caused her cheeks to feel so hot?

This wasn't like her, throwing herself at a man. She wasn't the type to go from man to man on a whim, or because she had some "needs" that demanded satisfying.

You've got needs tonight, a soft, taunting voice in her head insisted.

She did, and those needs seemed to be eating her alive.

Irena blew out a breath. Thank God Brody was so honorable. Another man would have probably dragged her inside and ravaged her after such an open invitation.

"You're right. I'll see you in the morning," she said, nodding.

"Right. Count on it." The words came automatically as he continued to struggle for control. "Now go inside," he instructed.

Go inside before I forget every decent thing I ever knew and make love with you until you forget you ever cared about Ryan.

He knew he shouldn't be thinking this way, given that his brother had just died, but that didn't make what he was thinking any less true.

Brody stood back, waiting until the only woman he'd ever loved closed the door behind her. For a second, he grappled with a renewed desire to follow her inside. Shoving his hands into his pockets, he turned on the heel of his boot and walked back to his vehicle, wondering if he was too old to receive a merit badge.

Did the Boy Scouts give one for gallantry and abstinence?

Eight o'clock the next morning found Brody back in front of Yuri's door, feeling not unlike thirty miles of bad road. Behind him, the sun was just struggling to rise. They still had almost twelve hours of daylight, but that was changing rapidly with each passing day.

He'd gotten very little sleep. Once in bed, he discovered that he was far too wired to fall asleep for more than a few minutes at a time. And whenever he did fall asleep, he wound up dreaming about those few wonderful moments in front of her grandfather's door. Not that reliving the kiss over and over again was a bad thing but it certainly wasn't conducive to restful sleeping.

Or any sort of ultimate satisfaction.

So here he was, with less than an hour and a half of sleep behind him, facing what promised to be a very full day of physical labor. He just hoped he wouldn't suddenly fall asleep while handling a power saw.

But he had to get to Yuri's place. He had a promise to keep.

Irena answered the door on the first knock. When she opened it, she looked incredibly refreshed.

"Sleep well?" he heard himself asking. Hadn't last night kept her awake at all? Had kissing him meant nothing to her?

Don't go there. You'll drive yourself crazy.

Irena smiled at him almost shyly. The truth was, she hadn't slept all that well. A mixture of guilt and adrenaline had conspired against her. But years as a law student and then a lawyer had taught her two things: how to get by on very little sleep and how to look good doing it. She was very resourceful when it came to applying makeup.

"Like a baby." She held the door open rather than grabbing her parka and stepping outside. "Would you like to come in for some coffee?"

"Coffee?" he repeated as if he'd never heard the word before.

Irena's mouth curved in amusement. There was something undeniably adorable about him this morning. It made her want to mother him and passionately hug him at the same time.

Her lack of sleep was making her a little crazy, she supposed.

"Yes, coffee. You know, that black, inky stuff that supposedly kick-starts a lot of us into our day? I just made a fresh pot, and I'd hate to see it go to waste." She opened the door wider in an unspoken invitation.

He remained where he was, as if his powers of resistance wouldn't work once he crossed the threshold. "What about Yuri and Ursula? Won't they take care of your 'surplus'?"

Yuri and Ursula were not your traditional grandparent types. They liked to stay up till all hours and, from what she'd gathered when they came to visit her right after their wedding, their appetites were all intact. Ursula had said that the wedding was Yuri's idea. She would have been perfectly happy to have lived with him without the benefit of clergy.

Irena glanced over her shoulder toward the staircase. "They came in at about two-thirty. I doubt very much that they'll be up anytime soon. The mail pouch doesn't come in today, so Ursula doesn't have a pressing reason to get to the post office before noon. By the time they get to the coffee, it'll be almost solid."

He knew it would be best to go. He shouldn't be alone with her.

"Thanks, but I've already had coffee." Which was true. He'd had several cups in an effort to wake up his system. "And," he said as he glanced at his watch, "I'm on a schedule."

"Right, the reservation," she said. Leaning into the

house, she grabbed her jacket from the hook just inside the door. "I remember."

Irena flashed a smile at him that he hadn't really seen up until now. Disarming, it went straight to his gut, settling in and taking him prisoner. He would have had a hard time getting through the next few days.

Leading the way to his vehicle, Brody opened the door for her, then closed it once she sat down.

Irena waited until he came around to her side before she said, "I really do appreciate this, Brody, you going with me to the funeral parlor."

He dismissed her thanks. He'd already told her it was unnecessary. "Don't mention it."

"And I meant what I said," she went on once he started up his car. "I want to help out at the reservation."

"You don't have to do that, either," he told her, keeping his eyes on the road. It wasn't traffic that he anticipated. Hades didn't experience traffic problems no matter what time of day. But the occasional moose or deer still wandered into town and he would have hated hitting one of them. On a day like today, given his lulled reflexes, he knew he had to remain extra alert.

"Yes, I do," Irena insisted firmly. "It's the least I can do in exchange for your going with me to the funeral parlor. And besides, I like being busy."

Brody quietly sighed and shook his head. "I'm not going to argue with you."

"Good, because you wouldn't win." She grinned. "Don't forget, I argue for a living."

He laughed then. "You couldn't have picked a better vocation if you tried."

The sound of her laughter in response was like music to him.

Allen Brothers Funeral Parlor was one of the oldest buildings in Hades. It was also one of the smallest. Given the town's population, however, the size was adequate. Nathan Allen, the thirty-year-old grandson of the original proprietor, had even sold off the eastern side of the wooden building to his Aunt Jennie, his father's older sister. Jenny Allen turned the small space into a flower shop, supplying flowers for the graves and, on occasion, bouquets to be bought by smitten young men for the objects of their affections. Competition for women was an ongoing endeavor in Hades, even with the increased influx of new citizens.

The building smelled musty, Irena thought as she entered quietly. As musty as it had smelled the day she'd walked in, clutching her mother's hand, to see her father laid out in a coffin. That was the last time she'd been inside the funeral parlor.

A feeling of déjà vu slipped over her.

But there were some differences.

Unlike with her father, the coffin wasn't open this time. Brody had warned her about that. The lid was firmly closed, making one last glimpse of Ryan a foregone impossibility.

Her heart ached in her chest as she approached. The words, "What if?" echoed over and over again in her brain like a needle stuck in a groove of an old-fashioned record.

Feeling as if she were moving in slow motion, Irena cautiously approached the coffin. After a beat, she raised her hand and ran it along the smooth, highly polished wood. Ryan was in there. Or what was left of him. His shell.

As if in a trance, she feathered her fingers along the edge of the lid. And then she slowly began to raise it.

The next moment, Brody had his hand over hers, pressing it gently down again. "You really don't want to do that," he whispered against her ear.

"Yes, I do," she answered, turning her head to look at him. "Brody, I need to say goodbye."

Continuing to keep his hand on hers, he slowly moved her hand from the lid. "You did that ten years ago," he reminded her. "Keep that image in your head," he urged. "The way Ryan looked then. You don't need to see him the way he wound up. The way I had to see him," he added solemnly.

It was going to take him a long, long time to get that image out of his head, Brody thought. And a long time for him to shed his anger and forgive Ryan for the terrible, wasteful thing he had done.

Brody saw the struggle in her eyes. Saw that the moment he withdrew his hand, she would open the lid. He couldn't let her do it. As much as he would grant her anything, this one thing he couldn't allow her to do. For her own sake.

"Do it for me," he urged quietly.

For a moment, Irena wavered, the need to see warring with the need to remember. And then she nodded. His eyes remained on hers as he slowly lifted his hand away. He was leaving her on her honor.

Irena let her hand drop to her side.

"All right," she agreed in a subdued voice. "For you."

They remained a few more minutes, spending the time in silence. Brody waited patiently as Irena stood beside the coffin. Her eyes welled up with tears. Without a word, Brody offered her a handkerchief. She accepted it and dried her eyes, then handed it back to him.

Looking down at the casket, she exhaled a breath pregnant with emotion.

"Goodbye, Ryan," she whispered. Raising her head, she glanced at Brody. Forcing her mouth to curve in a small smile, she said, "Okay, let's go."

He took her arm without a word and ushered her out of the building. He heard her take in a deep, shaky breath the moment they were outside.

"Sure you want to come along?" he pressed, concerned how all this had affected her. "I can easily take you back to your grandfather's house." He nodded in the direction they'd come from.

Irena noticed that Brody hadn't offered to take her to her mother's old house, the house he'd helped get up and running. He didn't want her to be alone, she concluded.

Ever since she could remember, Brody had always tried his best to look after her. A warm fondness filtered through her.

"I'm sure," she assured him. And then she smiled at him, tucking both arms around his. "Besides, I want to see what you've been up to these last ten years."

The Irena he remembered would have understood, would have been part of what he was doing. But it had been ten years since she'd been gone. People changed a lot in ten years. He had no doubts that she had long since outgrown both him and Hades.

"Nothing earth-shattering," he answered. "Just doing my part."

"And everyone else's, if I know you," she added knowingly.

She knew for a fact that Brody had always felt he had to make up for both his father's and his brother's behavior, as if life was some kind of large ledger comprised of debits and credits and it was up to him to balance his family's ledger.

Brody Hayes had to be the most unselfish person she'd ever had the good fortune to know.

He shrugged off her words. He knew she meant them as a compliment, not a criticism, but attention had always made him uncomfortable.

"When I need to," he allowed. Brody glanced down at her hands. She had beautifully manicured nails, he thought again. There was a light sheen to them. She still didn't care for colored nail polish, he surmised. "You're going to be breaking nails as well as hammering them."

Irena grinned. The idea of hammering nails, of channeling some of the tension still humming inside of her because of her impulsive behavior last night, pleased her.

"That doesn't frighten me, you know," she informed him playfully, then raised her chin and tossed her hair over her shoulder. "I've never been afraid of hard work."

"What have you been afraid of?" The question slipped out naturally, but the moment it did, he regretted it. The question was far too probing.

To his relief, she didn't shut down or back away. Instead, she replied flippantly, "Not much." Then, in a more sober tone, added, "Except maybe having too much time on my hands."

He liked the feel of having her arms wrapped around his, even if there were bulky jackets in between. He liked having her close like this, if but for a moment. "And why's that?"

Damn it, if only she hadn't loved Ryan—didn't love Ryan...

She got into Brody's car and buckled up. "If I have too much time on my hands, I start to think, to second guess myself, to reexamine things, and there's really no point in that except to drive myself crazy." Brody started the car and she settled in. "No one wants to hire a crazy lawyer and I can't go back in time and change things."

"What things would you change if you could?" he asked.

She looked at his profile for a long moment. "Just things," she whispered under her breath.

He knew what he wanted her to mean by the comment—that she regretted not realizing that he loved her, that he was the one who would always be faithful to her, not Ryan. She probably meant that, given a second chance, she wouldn't have left Hades. Would have forgiven Ryan his wandering ways and tried hard to make him settle down.

Who knows, maybe it would have worked. But he had his doubts. And anyway, they'd never have any way of knowing.

They were on the road to the reservation now. Lapsing into silence, Irena looked around as Brody drove. Daylight brightened the desolate scenery.

Nothing had changed, she thought again. This was timeless. It would be this desolate long after they were all gone. There would be no—

Irena squinted, trying to make out if there was something up ahead. There was. It was another vehicle. Except that it was just sitting in the middle of the road, as if posing for a travelogue photograph.

Irena could see that someone was in the car.

"Who's that?" she asked, turning toward Brody.

"Not sure yet," he answered, stepping down on the accelerator.

It seemed like an odd place to just pull over, she thought. "Why isn't he moving?"

"That's what I intend to find out," Brody answered, then smiled at her. She was asking the same questions he was. "Looks like we still think alike."

"Looks like," she agreed. And for some reason, she realized, she found that oddly comforting.

Chapter Seven

As they drew closer, Brody recognized the hunched, tall, gaunt old man standing beside a truck. It was hard to say which looked the worse for wear, the old man or the truck he mournfully regarded. The man, Ed Fox, was one of the Kenaitze elders. The tribe's population was slowly dwindling.

Brody rolled down his window and called out, "Hi, Ed, anything wrong?"

Ed didn't even turn to see who was talking to him. All his attention was focused on the vehicle that had incurred his ire and displeasure. "Yes, something's wrong. The damn truck quit running."

Brody got out of his car to investigate. "You can stay here," he told Irena just before he shut the door.

"I could," she agreed as she got out on her side. It wasn't in her just to sit on the sidelines no matter what was going on. Especially not when the sidelines were cold. "But I won't."

Brody suppressed a smile. He'd known she would come out. The Irena he remembered never hung back.

He turned his attention to the old man. Ed was murmuring under his breath in his native tongue. From the expression on the elder's lined, weather-beaten face, Brody judged that Ed wasn't saying anything favorable.

Opening the truck's door, he climbed into the driver's seat. "I didn't know you had a truck, Ed." Brody turned the key in the ignition. A whisper of a noise greeted him. That was the sound of the engine *not* turning over, he thought, trying again. Same results.

Ed scowled. It was apparent to Irena that the old man didn't like being in a helpless position.

"I don't. I've got a piece of junk. Stupid new old truck," he spat out, kicking a tire.

Getting out, Brody opened the hood to investigate. The engine was filthy. There was a snowy substance around the battery terminals and an odd, acrid smell rising up to his nose. As an armchair mechanic, there was nothing going on here that he could adequately address. This was a job for a professional.

He closed the hood again and turned to the old man. "I could have it towed into town and have June take a look at it."

Ed's scowl deepened. "Don't have money for that," he replied. He appeared pained by the admission.

Brody shrugged off the response. "Don't worry about it."

The old man eyed him sharply. "I don't take no charity."

"I wasn't offering any," Brody said mildly. He knew the kind of pride he was up against. "We'll come up with a fair exchange." He took a step back to get a better view of the truck. Because of his interactions with the people on the reservation, he was aware of most of their vehicles. "When did you get this?"

Ed shoved his hands into his heavy sheepskin jacket. "Last week. Figured I needed a truck to get around." He frowned again. "Can't be depending on other people all the time. Finally got enough to go see a used car dealer in Anchorage." The tribal elder slanted a glance at the woman with Brody, but if he was curious about her, it didn't show. "He told me that this one was a honey." He made a disparaging noise. "Ask me, it's pretty sour for a honey."

"Anyone go with you?"

Pride hardened the leathery features as Ed raised his head. "Don't need anyone to hold my hand. I've been doing things on my own since before your daddy ever met your mama."

Brody gently tiptoed around the elder's pride. He knew how easily that could be damaged.

"I know, but sometimes it helps to have someone take a second view of things." He threw in a cliché for good measure. "Two heads are better than one."

"My head's just fine on its own," Ed informed him indignantly. "That guy at the lot back in Anchorage was a damn crook." He blew out a frustrated breath. "And I'm out five thousand dollars."

Brody appraised the dark-blue vehicle skeptically. He wasn't all that familiar with trucks, but he was vaguely aware of the fact that the model was somewhere around ten, fifteen years old. And it was in less than stellar condition. It wasn't worth half the money that Ed had paid for it.

He glanced toward the dashboard. The odometer was obscured. "How many miles are on it?"

Ed shrugged, as if that was of no consequence. "About 190,000. The salesman said that was a sign that it was a good truck," he added. "Because it's been going for so long." There was a defensive note in the elder's voice, as if he knew Brody thought he'd made a mistake in buying the truck. An opinion he now shared.

"What was his name?" Both men turned to look at Irena as she asked the question. "The salesman who sold it to you, what was his name?" she pressed.

"It was on the bill of sale," Ed finally said. He tried to recall what was written on the contract. "Phil something-or-other."

"Do you still have the receipt?" she asked Ed.

"Yeah." And then he paused, thinking. His tone was less hostile as he added, "Someplace."

She nodded, as if she understood how life could get away from you, leaving behind a not-too-neat trail of papers.

"Find it for me," she requested. "Maybe we can get 'Phil' to give you your money back."

For once the skepticism left the old man's face. In its place was surprise. "Really?"

Irena knew she was going out on a limb, but she also felt that she could deliver. Still, it was always wise to remain conservative. "I'm not making any promises, but…maybe," she concluded, smiling at the man.

"In the meantime," Brody said, opening the passenger door behind where Irena had been sitting, "we'll give you a ride back to the reservation."

Ed looked dubiously at the truck. It was obvious that he didn't want to leave it here like this. "What about my truck?"

"I'll call June once we get to the reservation. She'll have someone come out to tow it to her shop," Brody promised.

Ed nodded his approval of the plan. "Okay. Thank you," he added stoically.

Satisfied, the old man climbed into the backseat, wrapping himself up in a blanket of pride.

"Not that I don't think you can work magic," Brody began once they had dropped Ed off at his house on the outskirts of the reservation, "but just how are you going to get this Phil what's-his-name to give Ed his money back? This is a used car salesman we're talking about. They customarily have hides as tough as rhinos. He'll come back at you and say the sale was made in good faith."

To his surprise, Irena nodded her head in agreement. "Most likely."

Had she just said what she had to placate the old

man, to calm him down until he reconciled himself to losing his money? "Then what—?"

"That's what he'll say," she emphasized. "Doesn't mean that Phil-what's-his-name'll get away with it." She smiled serenely. "Especially if I threaten to hit him where it hurts."

He made a right turn at the fork in the road. "Meaning?"

"Meaning this Phil character relies on his reputation to continue making sales, especially in times like this. If someone were to, say, tell him that they planned to have all the local papers carry the story of how he took advantage of a poor Kenaitze elder, cheating him out of his hard-earned savings by misrepresenting the reliability of the truck he sold him, well, Phil-what's-his-name just might not want that to happen."

He could see the value of that. Moreover, he could see her doing it. Brody grinned, nodding his head. "Might just work." And then he regarded her for a second as he drove to the meeting place. "You know, you're sneakier than you used to be."

She took it as a compliment. "That's because I'm a lawyer now."

Brody laughed, shaking his head as he parked his four-wheel drive vehicle in front of the schoolhouse. Many of the tribal children still went here, choosing to remain with their own rather than to attend the elementary school in Hades.

He'd no sooner brought the car to a halt when several people emerged from the building. A tall, muscular and stately man who looked to be in his mid-thirties led the group.

"Thought maybe you changed your mind," he said to Brody by way of a greeting. Sharp eyes the color of coal slid over the woman next to Brody and swiftly made assessment. "See why you were late."

Brody glanced at Irena to see if the assumption bothered her. He was relieved to see it didn't. "Not so late," Brody pointed out.

"We stopped to pick Ed Fox up," she told him.

A hint of a smile settled on the man's lips. "Lucky Ed."

It was a nice smile, Irena decided, with no apparent agenda to it. "Not so lucky. The truck he bought is a lemon."

The other man shook his head, but his expression said he'd expected nothing else. "Told Ed to wait for me to go with him," he told Brody, "but that old man likes to walk his own path. Stubborn as hell."

Brody looked at him pointedly before saying, "A lot of that going around."

The smile transformed into a grin, softening the man's sharp features. "Yeah, but I'm always right." He turned toward her. "Matthew Long Wolf," he said, putting his hand out to her.

Irena slipped her hand into his, making sure her handshake was just as firm as Matthew's. "Irena Yovich," she responded.

Brody watched Matthew take more comprehensive measure of Irena. "Irena thinks she can get Ed's money back for him," he interjected.

"Really?" Matthew seemed impressed and laughed shortly. "You do that, the old man's going to adopt you."

Brody chuckled. "As if the man didn't already have enough trouble."

More people from the reservation were arriving to help out with the work. He felt heartened. When he'd first made his proposal to begin renovations three years ago, he'd been met with apathy. That was a thing of the past.

"C'mon," he urged Matthew, "daylight's burning and we've got a lot to tackle before it gets dark."

Matthew paused to look at Irena. "What're you going to do?"

"Anything that needs doing," she answered before Brody had a chance to respond for her. "Let's go."

Matthew glanced back at Brody for confirmation. "You heard the lady. Let's go."

"Don't have to tell me twice," Matthew said, picking up his box of tools.

The temperature never really became warmer than what it had been at sunrise. When she'd first arrived, Irena thought that it was chilly, but a few hours into the construction, she had worked up a good sweat. They all had, working pretty much for the duration of the day with only a few breaks, one of which was for lunch.

By the end of the day, she was certain she'd never worked so hard in her life. Or felt so good about it. At least emotionally.

Physically was another story entirely.

There was a considerable ache in her shoulders as well as her arms, the by-product of a combination of the different tasks she'd undertaken. She'd spent a good deal of her time swinging a hammer in one capacity or another. She'd also been one of the many who'd joined forces in order to raise the four skeletal-like sides of the house.

By the time the house was adequately framed, she was the closest she'd ever been to bone-melting exhaustion. It was a good tired, a fulfilled tired, even if her arms felt as if they each weighed a ton.

Finished for the day, Brody sought her out.

"You know, you could have quit at any time," he told her, dropping down beside her. About to take a drink, he paused and offered her the half filled bottle of water first.

She accepted it gratefully. Lifting her arm up was a challenge, but she managed, taking two long swigs before handing the bottle back to him.

"I don't quit," she answered with finality in a voice that was fairly hoarse from shouting. The nonstop din all around her had made regular conversation all but impossible—unless the other person was standing on top of her. She nodded at the bottle. "Didn't take you for the water bottle type."

"Water's from the spring," he told her. "I just filled it up."

"No wonder it tastes so good," she murmured.

Putting the bottle into the backpack he'd brought with him, Brody allowed himself a moment to study her. "You look bushed," he commented.

Irena wasn't about to have him tell her she'd gotten soft. "I'm ready to go," she protested, rising to her feet.

He remained sitting. "We're done for the day," he told her.

"Oh, thank God." With a sigh that went straight down to her toes, Irena literally collapsed back down on the makeshift bench.

She was just as scrappy, just as determined as ever, he thought. It was one of her traits that he'd always found endearing. Hell, everything about her was endearing.

"You know," he said in a conspiratorial voice, "it's okay to admit when you get tired."

Irena looked around at all the people, all the men, women and in some cases, children, who had spent the better part of the day, if not all of it, working, framing a house for one of their own. They were going back to their own homes now after taking the time to help someone else.

"None of them stopped," she said, nodding toward the dissipating group of people.

"They're used to physical labor," he pointed out. "You're not."

She raised her chin, only partially pretending to take offense. "I held my own."

"And then some," he agreed, a smile playing on his lips. He glanced down at her hands. "Too bad the same thing can't be said about your nails."

Irena looked down herself. She'd been too busy to notice their condition. She'd chipped almost all of them. "They'll grow back." Somewhat self-conscious, she curled her fingers into her palms. "I was going to file them down anyway."

"To the quick?" he teased.

Irena shrugged indifferently. "I hadn't decided yet."

She was adorable, he thought, then silently chided himself. He had to stop thinking like that. That way laid only frustration. He changed the subject. "You really think you can get Ed his money back?"

"Pretty sure." She'd learned that it wasn't wise to write anything in stone. Even sure things had a way of blowing up on you. But that didn't stop her from stubbornly trying to deliver. She smiled up at Brody. "If I can't, you can always go and threaten to beat salesman Phil up."

"Small problem with that," he informed her. "I don't believe in violence."

"You never got in a fight?" she asked, curious.

He didn't answer immediately, debating how much he wanted to share. "Just once," he finally said.

Despite what Hades was like, she fully expected him to confirm that he'd never exchanged blows with anyone. That he had caught her off guard. She couldn't imagine him angry enough to lose control.

"Oh? With who?" she asked. "Must have been pretty serious."

He looked at the setting sun, watching the rays retreat from the sky. "Seemed so at the time."

There was something in his voice that told her to go slowly.

"Tell me," she urged quietly.

He shook his head, still avoiding her eyes. "Maybe some other time."

The reticence hurt more than she thought it would. Then again, she had no right to show up ten years later and expect to resume their friendship just the way she'd left it.

"All right, I won't pry—even though I'd like to," she couldn't help adding.

They sat in silence for a few minutes as the sun all but extinguished itself. He supposed, after all this time, it didn't matter if he said something. It was all behind him. And Ryan was gone.

"I got into it with Ryan."

His answer surprised her. She'd known that Ryan had a temper, but he'd been fond of saying he was a lover, not a fighter. And she just couldn't picture Brody exchanging blows with his brother.

"Why?"

"Doesn't matter." He shouldn't have said anything.

"Sure it does if it was enough to get you to take a swing at your brother," she insisted. "Or was it the other way around?"

"No, I was the one who took the first swing," he admitted.

It was like pulling teeth, but Brody'd come this far; she wasn't about to let him just drop the subject. "Because…?"

He blew out a breath. "Because when you left, I told Ryan he was an idiot for letting you go. He didn't like me criticizing him. His answer was that no woman was irreplaceable, not even you." He saw the look that came into her eyes. He'd opened up wounds. "I knew he didn't mean it—"

"If he hadn't meant it," she said, her voice steely calm, "he would have gone after me." The smile on her lips held no humor. "It wasn't as if I dropped off the face of the earth." Her eyes shifted to Brody's face. "When Ryan said that, is that when you hit him?"

"Yeah," he admitted. "I lost my temper. It was a dumb thing to do."

She touched his face. "You were being my champion even when I wasn't there." She didn't deserve his friendship. "I'm sorry, Brody."

She dropped her hand from his face. Something inside his gut sank a little. "Sorry? About what?"

"That I lost touch with you. Just because I was angry with Ryan is no excuse not to answer your letters."

He shrugged, absolving her. "You were busy starting a new life."

"And I wanted to sever ties with Hades," she said honestly. "But if you'd have come out to visit me, I wouldn't have slammed the door in your face."

He'd actually thought about it once or twice, each time coming to the same conclusion. That there was no point in torturing himself. That he needed to move on. Except that he really hadn't.

"I would have reminded you of Ryan," he said matter-of-factly. "I didn't want to cause you any more pain than you already felt."

"You're one of a kind, Brody Hayes. And I have missed you," she told him with feeling. "Missed you a great deal."

Not half as much as I've missed you. "So maybe this time, we'll stay in touch," he said lightly, although he had his doubts they would. Once she went back to Seattle, she'd forget all about her time here.

"Maybe," she agreed. "Speaking of touch, would you mind working the knots out of my shoulders?" She turned her back to him, taking his answer for granted. "If they get any stiffer, June and Kevin's planes could land on them."

"Sure, no problem." Positioning himself behind her, Brody began to knead her shoulders. "You weren't kidding, were you? Your shoulders feel like rocks."

"Skip the flattery. Just massage," she instructed.

"Yes, ma'am."

She heard the smile in his voice, and it made her smile as well.

Brody could always make her smile, she thought fondly.

Chapter Eight

"You were serious, then," Brody remarked, glancing at her as she carefully folded the paper that Ed Fox had just given her.

Dead tired as they left the reservation, she'd still reminded Brody that they needed to stop at the elder's house before driving back to her grandfather's. If she was to get Ed's money back for him from the dealer, she needed to have the bill of sale for his defunct vehicle.

It took her a second to process Brody's statement. "About trying to get Ed's money back? Yes, I was serious. I don't lie to people just because it might be expedient. Lies," she said softly, "have a way of ambushing you when you're least prepared for them." Like

Ryan's had finally ensnared him, she added silently. Irena frowned slightly. "I thought we already settled that."

"We did," he answered, "but with all that you did today…" He'd actually thought that she'd forgotten all about her promise to the elder.

"No more than you," she pointed out.

He continued as if she hadn't said anything. "I thought that maybe you felt you'd given enough of your time."

Maybe she was just too tired, but she didn't follow his reasoning. "One thing doesn't have anything to do with the other, except maybe in the very broadest sense because they both involved people from the Kenaitze tribe." Irena tried unsuccessfully to stifle a yawn. "Sorry, I think I really am bone tired."

He'd watched her today. Given the fact that she spent her time behind a desk and in court, he was really surprised at how hard she could work. Some of the others who had joined in on today's effort had gone home long before she'd finally surrendered to fatigue and agreed to stop.

"That makes two of us," he told her. "If you want to know the truth, I'm having trouble just keeping my eyes open."

"Not exactly reassuring to hear, given that you're the one who's driving." She took a breath, pulling herself together. "You want me to take the wheel?"

Brody shook his head. She looked far too tired for him even to consider her offer. "Your eyes are drooping, too."

She opened her mouth to protest, then shut it again.

There was no point in arguing with him. She wasn't any more wide awake than he was, possibly less. She was accustomed to burning the midnight oil, but there was never any heavy lifting involved.

"Maybe we should have stayed at the reservation," she told him, thinking out loud. "Somebody could have put us up for the night. Or, worse come to worst, we could have spent the night in the schoolhouse."

The suggestion was not without merit. And the idea of spending the night with her anywhere fired his imagination. With effort, Brody reined in his thoughts.

"Not a bad idea," he said, trying to sound detached. He kept his eyes on the road, which was illuminated by the car's headlights. "I'd turn around, but we're already past the halfway point." And then, as he remembered something, he turned the wheel sharply to the left.

Irena's eyes flew open—when had she closed them? She had to brace her hands on the dashboard to keep from falling into Brody.

"What?" she cried, confused and trying to look through the windshield beyond the high beams. "Did you just miss a deer?"

The talk about taking shelter somewhere had reminded him of something. "No, I'm turning off for your parents' house. It's a lot closer than Yuri's place, and I did get it ready for you. Might as well get some use out of it," he told her.

She hadn't even thought of that. Irena shifted in her seat. Tired as she was, something stirred within her. Something very basic and almost primal. She did her best to ignore it. "You want to stay there tonight?"

"Unless you have some objection."

Stopping the car, Brody turned on the overhead light and looked at her. Was it his imagination, or was there a wariness in her eyes? Or was that just a reflection of his own uneasiness? Uneasiness because he felt as if he were willingly crossing the threshold to uncharted territory.

There was nothing to be uneasy about, he silently insisted. He was in complete control, the way he always was. That meant that his emotions wouldn't get the upper hand.

And neither would temptation.

"If you'd rather not…" He began, intentionally letting his voice trail off. Waiting for her to either agree, or tell him she'd rather keep going until they reached Yuri's house. Either way, he realized that he didn't feel exhausted anymore.

"No, of course not. Why shouldn't I want to spend the night at the old house?" Since she was agreeing, he turned off the overhead light and began driving again. He noticed that she knotted her fingers together in her lap. "It's a perfectly good idea," she continued. Was she convincing herself or him, he wondered. Or was he just reading too much into it? "Neither one of us is liable to hit another car, but that still doesn't mean we wouldn't drive into a tree or some other obstacle that might be out here. Besides," she concluded, turning toward him, the corners of her mouth curving, "why let all your hard work go to waste? I should spend at least one night in the old house."

She meant every word she had just said to him. So

why was her blood surging so enthusiastically through her veins at the prospect of spending the night in close proximity to Brody?

She had to be tired. And maybe just a little giddy.

Abruptly, she realized that they'd arrived at their destination. Taking out her cell phone, Irena looked at its face in the light coming from the interior of the opened car. There was a signal, she noted, but it was fairly low. As she began to press numbers, she saw the quizzical look on Brody's face.

"I'm leaving a message for my grandfather so he doesn't wonder where I am," she explained.

It felt odd, having to clock in after being on her own for so long. Odd, but at the same time, rather nice.

Having someone care where she was made her feel warm inside.

Instead of the answering machine picking up, the way she'd assumed, Irena heard heavy breathing and then Ursula's voice.

"Hello?"

It was on the tip of her tongue to ask the older woman if she was all right, but at the same time, she knew Ursula would take offense. Ursula was extremely touchy when it came to questions regarding her health.

So instead, she just said what she'd called to tell her grandfather. "Ursula, it's Irena. Brody and I decided that we're both too tired to drive all the way back to town. We're staying at my parents' old house. Tell Grandpa not to worry."

"He won't." A chuckle followed the somewhat labored

assurance. "See you two in the morning. Or whenever," Ursula cheerfully added, then terminated the call.

Leaving Irena staring thoughtfully at her silent phone.

Brody stopped short of the front door. "Something wrong?"

"No." She looked up as she tucked the phone away into the back pocket of her jeans. "I think I might have interrupted them." She didn't elaborate what she was thinking, but she doubted that she had to. "She sounded awfully breathless."

Brody laughed. "They are a pretty lusty pair," he agreed. "Ike told me that he'd happened on them a few times when they were 'indisposed,'" he said delicately.

That didn't make any sense. Why would Ike just walk in on her grandfather and Ursula like that? "In their house?"

"No. Yuri's truck. Other places." He grinned. "They're like a couple of teenagers who can't get enough of each other." And he knew that they were both aware of how lucky they were to have found one another. "More power to them."

It took her a second to reconcile herself to the idea of her grandfather and Ursula behaving like adolescents, but once she did, she smiled. She was glad for them. Life should be enjoyed whenever possible. Her grandfather had been alone for a very long time. He deserved whatever happiness he found.

"Amen to that," she murmured.

Walking in, she felt around on the wall for a light switch and turned it on. Bathed in muted light, the house seemed cozier now than it had when she'd first arrived.

As she looked slowly around, Irena felt far more wide awake. Wide awake with anticipation dancing through her, hard and fast. She was aware of every single nerve ending in her body.

Shrugging out of her parka, Irena draped it on the hook next to the door just the way she had when she was a little girl.

Memories, all jumbled up and intertwining, came rushing back to her, crowding her mind, stirring things inside of her. Alienation warred with a sense of belonging. She was an outsider and a native all at the same time.

Her eyes shifted toward Brody. More feelings surged inside her. Old feelings disguised as new ones. She searched for an inner calm, but it eluded her.

"Do you want to go straight to bed?" The moment the words were out of her mouth, she flushed. It sounded like a blatant invitation. "I—I mean—"

"I know what you mean," he laughed softly, lightly brushing his hand along her shoulder.

It was meant to be a reassuring, comforting gesture, but felt like more.

Brody stopped mid-stroke, his eyes hypnotically held by hers. Why did she have to be so beautiful? Just looking at her made him ache. He had to get past that.

"I thought maybe we could sit around for a while and just talk, like we used to. When we were kids." Each word seemed to come to his tongue slower than the one before.

"We're not kids anymore."

She didn't know what made her say that. It wasn't something that needed pointing out. Was she trying to tell him something? Or was it herself she was talking to?

"I know," he replied quietly. "Doesn't mean we can't talk."

"No." She couldn't seem to pull her eyes away from his lips, watching them as they moved. "It doesn't."

She stood as close to him as a heartbeat. She could feel his breath on her face when he spoke. The feel of his breath on her skin stirred her.

Was she just being needy again?

Was she missing Ryan, struggling to put his memory to rest? Struggling to accept that he was permanently out of her life?

No, it wasn't that. She'd made peace with all that. This was something different; although, if her very life depended on it, she wouldn't have been able to identify what.

Maybe she took after her grandfather, Irena thought cryptically. But she'd never needed to make love for its own sake before. It had to be something more, have some underlying factor beyond just the physical need. She needed an emotional connection.

Her head ached from trying to make sense of what was happening to her.

All she knew was that she was very, very attracted to the man she had always considered her best friend. Was this something new? Or something old? Something that had existed under the layers, away from the light of day and examining eyes?

Had it been there all along, waiting to be discovered? Had she kept it buried all this time?

She had no answers.

Except she did have an incredible need to connect with this friend from her past. This man who, within the space of a few hours, she'd come to admire and respect all over again.

She'd always known that Brody Hayes was a good, decent person who believed in helping his fellow man or woman whenever he could. Maybe she'd even taken it for granted. But her feelings, her admiration, had been strongly reinforced by the actions she'd witnessed since she'd arrived.

Right now, she found that irresistibly sexy.

Irena blinked. Was she losing her mind? Or just her inhibitions? She really couldn't say. And she'd deal with it later. Much later. Right now, there was a fire that needed putting out. And there was only one way to do that.

"Kiss me, Brody," she whispered, then repeated more urgently. "Kiss me."

The entreaty slipped warmly against his skin, melting into his flesh. A man could only resist for so long, could only hide behind crumbling noble intentions for just a limited amount of time.

And his time was up.

Brody felt his resolve disappear. With effort, he managed to scrap together a single protest. But it died after he'd uttered only the first word.

"Irena—"

Died because she'd brought up her mouth to his and held onto his shoulders.

That was all it took.

The feel of her lips on his terminated any fledgling notion that he could actually walk away from her. That he could continue his stoic behavior, reacting to her on a neutral plain, as if she was just his friend and nothing more. That she hadn't filled more than her share of his dreams, night after night. Though he might have tried to lie to her, to himself, there was absolutely nothing neutral about the way he felt about her, even at the very beginning.

Working alongside of Irena today had plainly shown him that. Just looking at her had caused his body temperature to rise several degrees, even as the day grew progressively colder.

Fantasies crowded his brain, ushered in by desire. Then, as well as now.

Especially now.

Because they were alone. Together. Isolated from everything and everyone else in the world. The star-filled night cloaked them in invisibility. And in anonymity. There were no rules, which meant that there were none to break and hold them back.

Brody felt on fire.

His mouth still sealed to hers, he ran his hands slowly, lovingly along her body, as if to memorize every inviting curve, every small dip.

His heart hammered harder and harder.

Dazed, aroused, Brody hardly remembered peeling away her clothing. One minute she was pressed against him, wearing jeans and a pullover, a fuzzy, deep-blue sweater, the next minute, all those items were on the floor and she was against him again, achingly nude.

He was aware of, in minute detail, the feel of her hands tugging, pushing, at times ripping his clothes from his body. That would forever be etched into his brain. Something to relive long after she had left his life again.

He didn't want to think about that, didn't want to think beyond this exquisite moment. She was in his arms and that was all that mattered.

Over and over again, Brody slanted his mouth over hers, kissing her lips, anointing her throat, reverently worshiping the swell of her breasts.

He felt his control slipping away by inches.

Brody lost himself in the taste of her, in the scent of her. Like a man finally allowed to give in to and revel in his addiction, Brody still couldn't get enough of her.

Struggling to rein himself in, he was afraid that he could hurt her or frighten her if the full measure of his want were allowed to emerge. But it grew increasingly difficult to keep even a little of himself in check.

He wanted to possess her, body and soul.

He knew he never could.

Irena just couldn't seem to catch her breath. She felt as if someone had scrambled her thoughts. There were no words to describe what she was feeling. She didn't know that it could be like this, that she could be gripped tightly by such a sweet agony.

An urgency vibrated through her, but she had little opportunity to do anything but react to the army of sensations assaulting her from every conceivable direction.

Brody's mouth was quick, clever, as it teased her into one spiraling climax after another, each different than the last. Not more, not less, just amazingly, exquisitely different. He'd brought his lips to her very core, then sought out new hidden points of pleasure. The back of her knee, the hollow of her throat, the space inside her elbow. Everywhere and anywhere turned into another cauldron of sensations, stirred into a frenzy by him.

She was exhausted beyond all human measure, yet still eager. Eager for more even though she couldn't begin to imagine how there could be more.

This was Brody? her brain demanded when it could form a coherent thought. Quiet, steadfast Brody? What kind of blinders had she been wearing all these years?

And then, as if to confirm that this was indeed her childhood confederate, the boy then man she had told all her secrets to, had trusted with her innermost thoughts, Brody was suddenly over her.

His eyes were smoky as he looked down at her.

Irena felt her heart embrace him with a fierceness that took away what little breath she had left. Her eyes on his, she parted her legs beneath him, issuing a silent invitation.

Her arms encircling him, Irena urgently whispered his name as she felt him enter. And then he began to move, first slowly, then with a rhythm that increased with every second that passed.

Her head spinning, Irena arched her hips, drawing him in farther. Stifling a moan, she began to mimic his movements. The tempo rose, becoming increasingly frantic.

And then the stars exploded, raining down in a bright, fiery display that would have robbed her of her last ounce of breath—if she'd had any left.

Chapter Nine

As the euphoria of lovemaking slowly ebbed, Irena realized that she was acutely aware of everything around her. Of the low moan of the wind outside her window. Of the sound of her own shallow breathing and the rhythm of Brody's heart as it beat erratically beneath her palm.

What was going through his head? she wondered. Was he as surprised as she was at what had happened? Did what they had just done completely change the way he regarded her?

God, she hoped not.

Despite the fact that she had allowed their relationship to lapse, Brody's friendship meant the world to her. She knew that now.

Lying beside him, she closed her eyes for a moment, searching for the right words. When she opened them again, she said, "I'm not like this, you know."

Her words warmed him, like a match that had been struck, giving light and heat to the darkness. Without realizing it, he tightened his arm around her.

Don't get carried away. This isn't going to go anywhere, he warned himself. Out loud, Brody said, "I know."

"I was engaged once." He probably thought she was rambling, but she really needed to make him understand that what had just happened here wasn't business as usual for her. That it was different from anything she had ever done before.

Engaged. He hadn't known that. A flicker of jealousy rose, then vanished. She'd said "was" not "is." It was in the past. That meant she was free. Tension receded.

"What happened?" he asked her.

"It didn't work out." It was a simple answer for a very complex occurrence. "I didn't know what I was looking for, what I wanted," she confessed, then sighed deeply. "I suppose that I just wanted to have someone to love."

Brody turned his head toward her. She was lying too close for him to see her expression. "And did you? Love him?" he pressed when she didn't answer.

"No." She searched for a way to make herself clear. "When I was with him, really with him," she emphasized, not wanting to use the words *making love* because she realized, looking back, that love hadn't been involved in the relationship at all, "I didn't fly."

"The way you did with Ryan," he guessed.

"The way I did with Ryan," she confirmed quietly. "I was certain that would never happen to me again, that I would never encounter that teeth-jarring, mind-boggling sensation ever again. That I'd never fly again." Irena raised herself up on one elbow in order to look down onto Brody's face. "If you're interested, just for the record, I flew tonight."

He felt himself wanting her all over again. Love all but squeezed his heart in two. Brody threaded his fingers through her hair, framing her face with his hands. Loving her more than he thought was humanly possible.

"I'm interested," he murmured. "Since we're sharing bits and pieces of our souls," he continued, measuring out each word, "maybe I should tell you that—"

Irena shook her head, the ends of her hair brushing seductively against her bare shoulder. She placed her finger to his lips, stopping him. "Don't," she entreated softly. "Don't say anything."

He was about to tell her that he'd wanted to make love with her for a very long time, that she had just fulfilled a very dear fantasy for him, but in the face of her words, he kept his silence.

"Why not?"

She released a shaky breath. "Because I'm very unclear about things right now. And I'm not someone who can offer anyone a tomorrow."

Brody laughed dryly. "Channeling Ryan?"

It wasn't like that. Ryan had wanted to have the most amount of fun—strings free—that he could. That wasn't her goal; it never had been. "Being wary of the feelings I had for Ryan," she corrected.

Brody's expression grew somber. "I'm not Ryan," he told her.

"I know that," she replied with feeling. She really admired and respected Brody. That could never have been said about the way she'd regarded Ryan. "You're kind, selfless, generous."

Brody frowned slightly, even as he was acutely aware of her nude body leaning against his. "You make me sound as boring as oatmeal."

She smiled at him, her eyes crinkling. "Oatmeal never made me fly."

Mentally, he clung to that, knowing that however this turned out, they'd shared this moment together. And then he grinned at her. He'd been on the receiving end of far more than he had ever thought he would be.

Reaching up, he toyed with her hair. "Would you like to try for a round trip?"

Her eyebrows rose, disappearing beneath the tousled hair that dipped down into her eyes. "So soon?"

"Soon is a relative term. Besides, there's no time like the present," he replied just before he brought her mouth down to his.

Fire reentered her veins.

Irena woke up before dawn stirred and brought light to chase away the darkness. She felt both energized and more confused than ever as she hurriedly got into her clothes. The feelings she experienced were not the kind a woman had for her best friend.

It would be best for everyone if she could just dial her feelings back a bit. Easier said than done. Just how do you unring a bell?

She couldn't. So she did the next best thing. She pretended that the bell had not been rung.

Dressed, she stood by the door, ready to go. "Think I can get June or Kevin to fly me to Anchorage this morning?" she asked Brody.

Opening the door, he waited for her to walk out first. Her casual question created a knot in his stomach. *What did you think? One time in bed with you and she'd just jump into your arms forever?* "You're leaving?"

Was that disappointment in his voice? Or was she just projecting her own feelings onto him? "No, I'm going to see the dealer who sold Ed his clunker, remember?"

Relief flooded through him, even though it made no logical sense to feel like this. She was still going to be leaving in a few days. Sunday was just around the corner and then she'd be gone out of his life again.

Unless he could find a way to talk her into staying.

He knew that was what had happened with Ike and Marta, and April and Jimmy, as well as several of the other couples. Only intending on staying in Hades for a short time, they'd all postponed their departures until, eventually, the thought of leaving ceased to be a viable possibility.

No, Brody told himself, he couldn't do that, couldn't selfishly make Irena remain in Hades. She had a life in Seattle, a thriving career, and even though Hades could definitely use a competent lawyer, it was a given that she couldn't achieve the kind of money and success here that she could in Seattle.

Still, he could make the most of the time that was left. "Right. Ed. I forgot," he admitted. "Want some backup?"

She was surprised at the offer. "You're volunteering?"

After last night, he just wanted to be with her. It didn't matter where or what he was doing. "Never hurts to have someone in your corner," he told her. "Strength in numbers and all that. Besides, I think I'd really like to see you in action. I have a feeling it's an impressive sight."

A smile played on her lips. "You already saw me in action."

"All right," he amended, "I'd like to see you in action with your clothes on." It occurred to him that maybe, after last night, she was uncomfortable in his company. "Unless you don't want me to come with you," he qualified.

Well, at least that hadn't changed, she thought. Brody was as mindful of her feelings as ever. He might look a lot like his late older brother but Brody really wasn't like Ryan. She was beginning to appreciate this fact.

"Sure, why not?" she said. "You can protect me in case this Phil what's-his-name turns out to be a short-tempered behemoth who decides he wants to take a swing at me."

He doubted if anyone would want to do that after seeing her, but he kept that to himself. "Partial to knights in shining armor, are you?"

Just since last night, she thought. Out loud, she said, "Every time," punctuating her words with a wide grin.

Ursula nearly walked right into them as Irena opened the door to Yuri's house. On her way to the post office, the older woman abruptly took a quick step back to prevent a collision.

"Well, hello." She made no move to go. If she was a few minutes late getting to the post office, it was really of no consequence. And this was far more interesting. Ursula's sharp blue eyes swiftly raced over her husband's granddaughter and the young woman's companion. What she saw made her smile in triumph. "You're glowing," she announced with pleasure.

Instantly self-conscious, Irena said, "Cold air stings."

Ursula's smile deepened, causing her eyes to almost disappear into small crescent slits. "So does a hot bed."

Irena's mouth dropped open. "Ursula, please," she protested, embarrassment reddening her cheeks.

Hades' postmistress shrugged innocently. "Just making an observation," she pointed out. Leaning against the door, oblivious to the draft, Ursula glanced from Irena to Brody. Both looked as if they were in a hurry to get somewhere. She wasn't accustomed to seeing anyone hurry—unless it involved either a fire or a mine accident. "You two going somewhere?" she asked.

Irena had gotten out of the habit of announcing her schedule, but she didn't see the point in being rude, so she answered Ursula's question.

"I'm going to go change and then I need to see if I

can get Kevin or June to take me—us," she amended, "to Anchorage."

Thickened eyebrows drew together as Ursula took in what was being said. "You're not leaving, are you?"

Because he knew that Irena hated to take credit for good deeds, Brody answered for her. "She's going to make a car dealer tear up a contract he'd written in bad faith and get him to give a man his money back."

The sound of Ursula's throaty laugh echoed through the front room. She stopped when she saw the expression on Irena's face. "You're serious?"

Irena nodded. "Very."

Her response drew a very pleased smile from Ursula. The older woman patted her on the arm. "Yuri never mentioned that you were a scrapper. You go, girl," she urged. Then, glancing at her watch, she announced, "Well, I'd better woman my post." Ursula, apparently, resented the idea of having to "man" her post, Irena thought, amused.

Almost an hour later, she and Brody finally arrived at the air terminal. As they crossed the field and approached the tiny office, Irena saw Kevin emerge. He met them halfway.

"Got your plane all gassed up and ready to go," he called out to her. "And I'll only charge you just what it costs me for the gas, seeing as how you're championing one of our own."

Caught off guard, Irena stared at Kevin. "How did you—"

Grinning, he answered her question with a single word. "Ursula."

Irena shook her head. The woman had been in her company less than an hour ago. How did she manage to spread the word so quickly? "She's better than a newspaper."

"Much better," Kevin assured her. They had all learned to have a healthy respect for the older woman's ability to retrieve and disseminate information. "You have to read a newspaper. By the end of the day—if not before—everyone in Hades will have heard the story of how you took on a used car salesman and got one of the tribal elders his money back for him."

If she managed to accomplish that. She was fairly certain of her method, but nothing was guaranteed. Irena blew out a breath.

"No pressure here," she murmured quietly to herself—or thought she did.

"No more than you put on yourself," Brody interjected.

She turned to Brody. The man had a knack of reading her mind. She'd forgotten about that. "Let's go, Sancho."

"You don't have a beard and mustache, not to mention that you're definitely the wrong gender and age to be Don Quixote."

"Picky, picky, picky," she chided with a laugh as she fell into step behind Kevin as he escorted them back across the field to his plane.

Phil's last name turned out to be Daily. His warm greeting and two-hundred-watt smile faded instantly when he realized that the young couple on his lot had no intention of buying any of his "pre-owned" vehicles and had, instead, come about one of his recent sales.

He obviously had a sharp mind given to retaining an endless amount of details. He seemed to recall the transaction in question the moment he was shown the sales receipt. He shook his head, as if suppressing his annoyance over Irena's polite request for reimbursement.

"Currently, the truck is at a garage in Hades where it was towed. To get it up and running would cost more than the truck is worth." She'd checked with June about that before she'd taken off. "I can give you the address and you can make arrangements to bring it back to your lot—if you want to go through that trouble."

"Why would I take a truck that's not mine?" Phil asked innocently. And then his manner grew slightly more belligerent. "That sale was final." He glanced down at the receipt. "Mr. Fox knew what he was getting."

Irena took exception. She hated people who took advantage of others with a passion. "I doubt very much if Mr. Fox knew he was getting a truck whose engine was on its way out and whose starter had only a few more 'starts' left in it before it stopped living up to its name."

Daily shrugged indifferently, dismissing the truck's shortcomings. "Not my problem."

The salesman started to leave his small office. Brody rose from his seat and silently placed his hand on the other man's chest, his meaning clear. Daily wasn't going anywhere until this was resolved to Irena's satisfaction. Anger colored the salesman's face, but he remained where he was, no doubt recognizing his folly.

"Oh, but I think it is your problem," Irena informed

him in a quiet, firm voice. Having Brody with her made this a great deal easier, she thought. Otherwise, she had a feeling she would have had to follow Daily around the lot as she made her point.

Daily scowled at her, grudgingly returning to his desk. He sat down, but he was still very defiant. "And just how do you figure that?" he demanded. "The law's on my side."

"The law might be," she allowed in the same easy cadence, noting with satisfaction that it was getting under the salesman's skin, "but it'll do you precious little good if the customers aren't."

Daily glared at her, ignoring Brody's presence. "And how do you propose to do that? You going to picket the lot?" he sneered.

"Only as a last resort. I don't imagine people are liable to do business with a dealership that preys on old, unsophisticated, trusting people, taking their money and leaving them literally stranded. Mr. Fox could have froze to death if we hadn't happened along when we did."

Okay, it was an exaggeration, she silently admitted, but it made her point and she wasn't above embellishing if it meant a victory for the old man.

Irena moved forward on her chair, her body tensing as she made her point.

"I intend to begin a letter-writing campaign, sending letters to every single periodical in this state as well as a few in Canada. In it I'll detail exactly how long Ed worked to scrape his money together in order to buy the lemon you sold him and how quickly the truck died once he had it off the lot."

Daily drew himself up. "I'll get a lawyer and sue you and that old man for libel," he shouted.

Brody stepped forward, but she put up her hand to stop him. Her gesture as well as her manner was filled with confidence. She could handle this.

"Libel implies that I'm lying. You and I both know I'm not." Opening her purse, she took out a card and placed it on the desk in front of the salesman. "And in case you're wondering, I *am* a lawyer." She sat back again, as relaxed as if she had already won this battle. "Trust me, Mr. Daily, you do not want to go up against me. I haven't lost a case in the last six years."

She rose to her feet, standing beside Brody. The latter continued to hold his peace, content just to observe her in action.

"It's all up to you," she informed Daily in a friendly tone that belied how she really felt about the man. "I've already drafted the letter on my computer. All I have to do is press Send and all the editorial sections of the major newspapers will have the story of how Ed Fox was cheated by a slick salesman. Even in this modern day and age, people still like rooting for the little guy." She deliberately held up the receipt in front of him. "In case you're unclear on the concept, that wouldn't be you."

Daily's face turned a deeper shade of red as he struggled with his anger. Rather than say anything, he snatched the receipt out of her hand, glanced down at the amount. Throwing it on his desk, he picked up the phone.

"Tina, I need you to cut a check for five thousand

dollars. Just do it," he snapped in response to the question the woman on the other end of the line asked.

"And three hundred," Irena added.

"What?" Daily demanded hotly.

"Five thousand three hundred," Irena told him calmly. "Mr. Fox has to pay the mechanic who towed his vehicle to the shop."

"And three hundred," Daily told the cashier, then slammed down the receiver. He exhaled an angry breath. "Satisfied?"

Daily's glare could have fried eggs, she noted, refusing to look away. "When I have the check and Mr. Fox successfully cashes it at his bank, yes, I'll be satisfied."

Just then, there was a quick knock on the door to Daily's office. The next moment, it opened and a young woman in tight jeans and a midriff-baring pullover entered. She held an envelope presumably containing a freshly cut check. Her small brown eyes shifted from Daily to Brody and then back again. Tina raised her eyebrows quizzically.

"Give it to her," Daily snapped, pointing at Irena.

Irena smiled as she graciously accepted the check. Opening the envelope, she glanced at the amount to make sure it was correct. It was. She slipped it back into the envelope. Only then did she say, "Nice doing business with you, Phil."

She was fairly certain that Phil mumbled his retort rather than shouted it as she and Brody left the office only because of Brody's presence.

They made a good team, she couldn't help thinking, as they walked out of the dealer's showroom.

Chapter Ten

"That was a nice bit of work," Brody commented as he held the passenger door of the rental car.

Irena smiled at him as she got in. "Thank you." She waited for Brody to get in on his side before adding, "I really hate people who think nothing of taking advantage of other people."

For a moment, he said nothing as he started up the vehicle. He couldn't help wondering if, consciously or unconsciously, she was including him in that group because, God help him, he knew he'd taken advantage of her last night. Advantage of the situation and the fact that she was so obviously vulnerable and willing. Had he been truly honorable, he would have found a way to keep them both under control. Would have found something to talk about until she fell asleep. Given how exhausted she'd been, that wouldn't have taken long.

But the minute she'd kissed him, he'd been a goner. There was no other way to say it. A weak goner who gave in to his own longings.

He shouldn't have. He was supposed to be stronger than that. He *was* stronger than that.

But now was not the time to ask if, deep down, she included him in that group of users, and it certainly wasn't the right time to apologize.

Brody merely nodded and stuck closely to the subject at hand. "Ed's going to be very happy to see that money back, not to mention the bonus."

Irena looked at him in confusion. She wasn't following him. "Bonus?"

"Bonus," he repeated, then elaborated, "The extra three hundred."

Maybe he hadn't been paying attention in the office just now. "No, that's for June and Kevin. They did have the truck towed to their garage, and June did do some diagnostic work on the vehicle. I know she'll probably argue about taking it, but I figured they should be reimbursed for their work."

"So do I," Brody agreed. "That's why I already took care of the bill before we left this morning." He realized he was pressing down too hard on the accelerator and eased his foot back. It felt strange not driving his car. "I gave June the money."

"Then the extra three hundred's yours, not Ed's," she concluded.

The slight move of his shoulders showed his indifference to the amount. "Ed can use that three hundred a lot more than I can."

As far as she could discern, Brody didn't have any sort of a regular job. Yesterday showed off his life's work helping others, organizing drives to bring food, medicine and clothing to those who needed a hand. Unless he was a great deal richer than she thought, his was not an endless source of money. He needed to think about himself once in a while.

"You can't just keep giving money away, Brody."

He spared her a glance as he wove through the city traffic. "Why not?"

"Because then you'll have nothing to live on yourself."

Brody laughed. "I'm a long way from that. Besides, I don't need much and right now, I've got everything I need."

Everything he needed, she thought. Which meant that there was no place for her in his life.

Of course there wasn't, Irena upbraided herself. Why should there be? She couldn't expect to have everything change in Hades just because she'd decided to come waltzing through. Besides, she wasn't staying. She had a life in Seattle and he had one here. She knew that last night when she'd all but thrown herself at him.

All? she mocked herself. *That had been a grand slam home run right over the fence.*

Last night was a one-time thing, not the start of a relationship, she argued with herself. She had to remember the rules of the game: No strings, no repeat performances and above all, no expectations.

"That's good to know," she replied quietly.

Something in her voice caught his attention. Brody tried to read between the lines, then told himself that he was better off just letting it go. There was no "between the lines," no hidden meanings. Last night was what it was. An exquisite, isolated incident. They had no future and he knew that. Torturing himself was just that: self-inflected torture. Irena still loved Ryan, had made love with him because he looked so much like Ryan and because she was vulnerable. There was no point in making anything more of it because there *was* nothing more.

Painful as it was, he had to remember that.

"You did it," Ed Fox murmured several hours later, staring at the check in his hands like a man in a trance. "You really did it." He raised his eyes to look at her. "You really got my money back." It was obvious from his tone that he hadn't actually thought it possible, despite her promise.

"I said I would," Irena reminded the older man.

They were inside the tribal elder's modest dwelling. Built out of wood decades ago, the house was sparsely furnished and she was acutely aware of a draft coming through, even though the windows and door were closed. She wondered if this house was next on Brody's project list. It was obvious that it needed major work. She couldn't help wondering if the elder's pride would interfere with that.

Ed looked at the amount again and then frowned ever so slightly. "This is far more than I paid," he protested, holding the check out to her. "I can't accept it."

"Of course you can," Irena countered, gently pushing

his hand back. "And the reason it's for more than you paid is because—"

"It's a bonus for pain and suffering," Brody interjected quickly, cutting off her explanation.

When she looked at him in surprise, the expression on Brody's face warned her not to go into any detail about his covering the repairs. They both knew that the tribal elder was not about to accept any charity.

"Pain and suffering?" Ed repeated slowly, as if examining each word separately to assess its meaning and worth.

"Legal talk for making that car salesman pay a fine for trying to cheat you," Irena told the man matter-of-factly, backing up Brody's story without missing a beat. Out of the corner of her eye, she saw Brody smile.

An expression of awe slipped over the man's lined face. "And you did this?"

Irena inclined her head toward Brody. "Actually, *we* did this."

Brody felt she was giving him too much credit. "You did the talking."

But he was her backup and ultimately that made the job easier for her. "And you were my silent muscle. That guy wasn't about to sit in his office and meekly listen to me. If it wasn't for you, I would have had to chase after him and follow him all around the car lot. It might have taken hours to get him to pay up."

The end result would have still been the same. "You would have worn him down." Brody had absolutely no doubt about that.

"That's beside the point," she said dismissively.

"Having you there to back me up made it that much easier. You saw the look on his face when he tried to leave and you put your hand on his chest to stop him. If I'd have done that, he would have run right over me."

The elder stepped in and terminated the back and forth discussion. "You are both very good people," he declared. His dark eyes shifted from one to the other. "We are very fortunate to have you helping us."

"Well, you're not going to have Irena for long," Brody replied, doing his damnedest not to sound as if her leaving wasn't going to bother him. "She and her silver tongue are going to be going back to Seattle soon."

Irena noted how matter-of-fact he sounded about her departure. If she didn't know better, she would have said he seemed eager for her to leave. Was he, at bottom, like Ryan after all?

Or was it that he viewed what happened last night as a mistake he shouldn't have made?

Irena suppressed a troubled sigh. She didn't know what to think. Didn't, truthfully, know what side she was rooting for anymore. Did she want him to want her to stay, or make it easy for her to go by not caring?

Why had life gotten so confusing?

The tribal elder eyed her with clear disappointment. "Soon?" he echoed the fatal word. "How soon?"

"Very soon," she replied, not wanting to say anything about leaving the day after the funeral. That subject wasn't one she wanted to open up for discussion. It was still far too personal.

"We will be sorry to see you go," Ed told her truthfully. "My son told me how hard you worked beside Brody yesterday. It is much appreciated," he added with feeling.

For a fleeting moment, her eyes met Brody's even though she was addressing her words to the old man. "I had something to prove." Then, she added whimsically, "I haven't gotten soft in 'the big city.'"

"Oh, I don't know, you felt pretty soft to me last night," Brody whispered into her ear, slipping one arm around her waist for a second, as if to underscore his statement.

If Ed Fox heard what Brody whispered, the man gave no indication. Instead, he asked her another question. "You will come back to the reservation before you leave?"

Irena hesitated for a moment. "When is your next house raising?" she asked Brody.

"Tomorrow. Friday," he added in case she had lost track of the days. It was an easy thing to do out here. With each day shortening a little more than the day before, sometimes he forgot what day of the week it was himself.

Irena smiled broadly at Ed. "Then, yes, I'll be back."

Brody didn't want her to feel obligated to pitch in. She'd already done far more than her share. "You don't have to."

"I know. I want to." Because Brody looked unconvinced, she added, "Might as well be useful while I'm here."

Why did she feel as if she had to be perpetually in motion? "Did it ever occur to you just to kick back and rest?" he asked.

"No." A trace of defensiveness entered her voice. "Did it ever occur to you?" she countered.

"No, not here." But that was because he'd dedicated himself to making the lives of both the people of the Kenaitze tribe and the local Inuits better. In effect, this was his job. His payment came in the form of satisfaction. "But if I went someplace for a visit—"

"I didn't come for a visit," she reminded him, then lowered her voice. "I came for a funeral. That's not quite the same thing."

He didn't want to argue with her. For whatever time he had left, he just wanted to enjoy her. "We'll take what we can get," he told her.

What he actually meant, he thought, was that *he* would take what he could get. When it came to Irena, expendable things like pride weren't allowed. A moment spent in her company was a moment he would cherish. Nothing else mattered to him.

Irena glanced at her watch. "Right now, we need to get me back to Hades. I promised my grandfather I'd spend some quality time with him before I have to go back to Seattle. I want to be sure I keep my promise."

"An honorable woman," Ed pronounced, nodding his gray head in approval. His eyes met Brody's for a moment before he crossed to the front door and opened it for Irena.

"Never thought of her any other way," Brody replied, placing a hand lightly against her elbow as he escorted her out.

"Even when Ryan and I were together?" she couldn't help asking, walking with him to his car. "Did you still think of me as being honorable then?"

He laughed softly. "Not only honorable but exceedingly patient and kind."

"I think the word that you're really looking for is 'stupid,'" Irena told him, getting in on the passenger side as he got in on his.

Their seat belts clicked simultaneously as they buckled up. "Why?"

Irena leaned back against the seat, closing her eyes wearily. "Because I believed Ryan when he told me that he loved me—"

This was where he could run down a list of all his brother's shortcomings, making her see that loving Ryan had been a mistake. But he couldn't do it. Couldn't make himself look better by making his brother look worse. Couldn't allow her to find fault in herself to gain his goal.

"I honestly think he did."

Whether or not Ryan loved her was only part of it. "And I believed him when he said he was being faithful to me."

Brody shook his head. He couldn't lie to make her feel better—because, in this case, she'd know he was lying. "Well, now, there you might have been a little myopic," he allowed.

"Not myopic, stupid," she repeated.

He wasn't going to have her beat herself up. Ryan could always be charmingly persuasive and his brother could manifest the sincerity of an angel when he wanted to.

"It's not stupid to believe in love, Irena. It's not stupid to want to believe that someone you love feels the same way about you as you do about him. You were faithful. You had every right to expect Ryan to be the same."

She shook her head. Brody didn't understand. "I didn't expect Ryan to be faithful, I *believed* him to be faithful. There's a difference. When you expect something from someone, in the back of your head you know there's a chance he might not deliver. But when you *believe* a person to be a certain way, that means that you're positive that he is. I actually believed that there was no one else in Ryan's life but me."

Staring out the window, Irena blew out a breath. Looking back, she shook her head, marveling at her own naïveté.

"I don't know what I could have been thinking. This was Ryan. Ryan the charmer. The guy who made every girl's heart skip a beat just by walking down the school hallway. I knew what he was like before he ever singled me out. And yet, for some reason, I thought I could make him want to change. I thought that he *had* changed. For me," she said sadly.

Talk about dumb, she thought.

"He should have," Brody told her. Which made his brother an idiot, because Ryan continued being what he was: a womanizer. "If Ryan'd had a brain in his head, he should have. The trouble with Ryan was that his philosophy had always been—so many women, so little time. And his ran out."

Brody glanced at her, noting how rigid her jawline was. She was trying not to cry, he thought. Damn it, Ryan never deserved her.

"If you ask me," he continued evenly, struggling to keep his feelings under wraps, "Ryan was the stupid one. Stupid for ending his life and even more stupid because he couldn't recognize how lucky he was, having you in his life."

She knew Brody was just trying to comfort her, but she appreciated it. "So just when did you develop this silver tongue?" she asked, a sad smile playing on her lips as she turned to look at him.

"If I sound as if I have a silver tongue, it's only because you bring it out of me. That, and I'm a quick study," he admitted. "Can't be around Ryan for all those years and not pick something up, even if you don't mean to."

With tears scrambling up the inside of her throat, Irena didn't trust herself to form an answer. She merely nodded her head as if in agreement, even though she was becoming more and more convinced that the only thing Ryan and Brody shared was a last name and some DNA. Otherwise, they were as different as night and day. And from where she stood, that was beginning to be a very good thing.

"It is being about time," Yuri said the moment she walked in.

Since she'd only spoken with her grandfather's wife this morning, Irena couldn't help but wonder just what kind of message Ursula had passed on to the old man.

She began at the beginning. "I'm sorry, Grandpa. I wanted to help Brody." Just as she said it, she heard the sound of Brody's car, driving away.

Yuri cocked his head as he looked at his granddaughter. "Brody?"

She could hear the flash of interest in her grandfather's voice, saw a knowing smile curve his mouth.

Had she just made a tactical mistake? Was he going to try to get more details out of her? Specifically about how she'd spent the night? God, she hoped not. Her grandfather was as tenacious as Ursula when it came to extracting information.

"Yes." She took off her parka. "He was going to the reservation to help them raise a new building."

"Brody is being a good man." He beckoned her over to the kitchen. Warm smells embraced her. Her grandfather loved to cook and there was bread baking in the oven. "And that was what you were doing today, too?"

Irena sat down at the table. "No, today I flew to Anchorage to see if I could get one of the tribal elders his money back from the unscrupulous car salesman who tried to unload a clunker on him."

Yuri took the bread out of the oven and set it on top of the counter to cool. Turning his attention to the coffeepot, he poured out two very inky cups of coffee and set one in front of her as well as one for himself. Rather than take his usual seat at the head of the table, he sat down beside her.

"Clunker?" he repeated. The word was obviously foreign to him.

"A used truck that didn't run," she explained.

"Ah." He nodded his head sagely. "And you are doing this, yes?"

"Yes." She took a sip from her cup, letting the warmth wind through her like the effects of a loving embrace. "I got him his money back."

"Good. Good." And then to her surprise, her grandfather took her chin in his hand, as if that could somehow help him study her. "But you are not happy," he concluded.

She drew her head back and he dropped his hand. "Of course I'm happy."

But he shook his head. "No, that is being a little happy. Something else is making you sadder." His eyes met hers. "Tell me."

He couldn't possibly know. He was just trying to break her by pretending he could delve into her thoughts, Irena insisted. She knew that, and yet, she could feel herself wavering.

"Grandpa, there's nothing."

Yuri refused to back off. "I am knowing this face of yours. I have been knowing it since you were being a baby. You cannot fooling me."

She stalled, drinking more of the coffee. The warm embrace eluded her. "I am not trying to 'fooling you,' Grandpa."

"Then it is yourself you are trying to fool?" he asked, concerned. Before she could make up an answer, he pressed, "What is being wrong, Irena? My English is not good, but my heart is," he went on, softly. "And my heart is knowing there is something wrong."

She blew out a breath, looking off through the window. It faced the wilderness. The vastness of it made her feel alone. She felt his rough hand covering hers, giving lie to her feeling.

"I'm just confused, Grandpa."

He waited, then coaxed. "About?"

"About where I belong."

Yuri smiled as he took her hands in his. "That is easy."

She fully expected him to say "here," but decided to let him tell her. Maybe, if he did, she might believe it. But she doubted it. "It is? Where, Grandpa? Where do I belong?"

Yuri stared at her for a long moment, as if he was peering into her soul, her thoughts. She knew it was all her imagination. And yet...

"You are belonging where your heart is. Because you cannot be doing without one," he added with quiet conviction.

The problem was she knew he was right. The bigger problem was she no longer knew where her heart really belonged.

Chapter Eleven

"Maybe," Yuri continued thoughtfully after a few moments had passed, "you are trying to being something that is not right for you." When Irena looked at him, he tried to explain more succinctly. "Maybe, what you are thinking you want is not what you are really wanting." And then he smiled his broad, crooked smile at her. "I am thinking you are needing to stay here a little longer to be making up your mind."

Irena saw through him. "You just want me to stay," she said fondly.

Her grandfather made no attempt to deny it. "I have never been saying anything else. But more than seeing your pretty face, Little One, I am wanting for you to be happy." Rising from the table, Yuri kissed her forehead. "And only you can be deciding what is making you that way."

What made her happy? That was the million-dollar question, Irena mused.

Lost in thought, Irena stared into the empty coffee cup as her grandfather's footsteps in the hallway grew fainter and fainter. She had grown up here and for eighteen years, like so many other native teenagers, all she could think of was leaving Hades. Of going off into the world and making her mark. She'd wanted to get away from the tiny town even before she discovered Ryan's infidelity.

And now, now she didn't know anymore. Being here had filled her with nostalgia, something she would have sworn wasn't possible—until she'd experienced it. For the last eighteen months or so, following her usual routine and working the long hours that were required had left her feeling burnt out. The wave of triumph after a victory grew shorter and shorter until it wasn't there at all.

Of late, she had been feeling unsatisfied. Purposeless and oddly hollow clear down to her toes.

She hadn't felt that way yesterday, she remembered. Working beside Brody and helping him and the others construct something meaningful—a place for a family to live—had filled that hollow feeling.

Granted what they had wound up building couldn't compare to her apartment back in Seattle, much less any of the many houses she'd been invited to these last few years. Houses belonging to the people she associated with as well as the people she successfully defended and their friends.

Her world was comprised of money and prestige.

Someone on the outside looking in would have said that she had it all. That she'd "made it."

Professionally, but not personally.

Wasn't it the same thing?

She'd once thought it was; now she wasn't quite so sure. From what she'd observed, she was fairly confident that Brody was far happier with his accomplishments than she was with hers.

Irena pressed her lips together, thinking of what she'd seen on the reservation yesterday. She hadn't realized it would be like that. Hadn't given it any thought, really. But seeing the poverty had been devastating. Children lived with this poverty every single day.

And Brody, well-intentioned Brody, could only give so much, do so much …

There was going to be a point, she thought again, when Brody was going to run out of money.

Unless …

Ideas began popping up in her head, crowding her mind. Suddenly, Irena didn't feel lost anymore. Maybe this wasn't the solution to what she wanted to do with her life, but her idea—if she was able to get positive responses—certainly would help Brody with what he was doing. And it would help a great deal more than just an extra set of hands for a few days. This could help him for an indefinite time to come.

Irena found herself grinning.

Inspired, she poured herself a second cup of coffee, then hurried into her room. Setting the cup down on the nightstand, for the first time since she'd arrived in Hades, she unpacked her laptop.

There were people she needed to get in contact with. People whom she could coax into making significant donations. Donations that would wind up helping to continue the fund what Brody was trying to accomplish.

Funding.

Foundation.

Thoughts raced through her mind, gelling rapidly. Of course. Why not form a foundation?

This time, when Irena took a sip of the new cup of coffee she'd poured, the feeling of a warm embrace was back.

She could hardly contain herself. Half a dozen times that day she caught herself reaching for the telephone. Once she even dialed straight through before she hung up. No, she wasn't going to tell him. Not until she sent out all the e-mails and had gotten at least one positive response.

The latter wasn't long in coming.

And she learned something.

At bottom, Irena realized as she read one e-mail after another, the people she associated with were a generous lot. They might be as competitive as hell, but given a worthy cause, their checkbooks came out. It was a way to painlessly give back a little of what they'd been blessed with.

She couldn't wait to tell Brody what she'd come up with. But this time, she didn't reach for the phone. She opted to do it in person.

Irena was up hours before the sun was, counting the minutes until Brody arrived on her doorstep. Neither

her grandfather nor Ursula were up yet when Brody came by to pick her up. She counted it as a merciful blessing.

Irena was outside, greeting him before his knuckles could made contact with the door. Brody dropped his hand to his side.

"Eager to get to work?" he guessed, amused. He noticed her eyes were actually sparkling. He could have spent the entire day just staring into them like a lovesick puppy.

Now there was a self-image he could do without. Brody forced himself to look away and lead the way back to his car.

"I've got some good news," Irena announced, addressing his back. It took a great deal not to shout out the words. The last e-mail she'd gotten this morning had brought with it an astounding pledge.

Opening the door for her, Brody quickly got in on his side. "You've decided to stay a little longer?" he guessed, mentally crossing his fingers. He turned the key in the ignition as she buckled up.

Brody's guess caught her completely off guard. Her mind, wound around this new turn of events, came to a skidding halt. She stared at him as he began to drive. Did that mean what she thought it did?

You're getting ahead of yourself again.

"Would you want me to?"

Brody laughed softly to himself and shook his head. "If you have to ask, Irena, then you're not as sharp as I thought you were."

"I'm considering that," she admitted, then, realizing

that her words sounded ambiguous, she said, "Staying a bit longer, not whether I'm sharp." She saw the grin emerging on his lips. Now it sounded as if she was bragging. Since when had she gotten so tongue-tied? "I mean—oh, don't confuse me, Brody."

"Never my intention," he told her innocently. He spared her a look. "Okay, so what's this good news you have to tell me?"

She took a deep breath, trying to get everything in order in her head and not just jump into the middle of it. She'd been dealing with e-mails and pledges for the last eighteen hours or so. She had to remember to begin at the beginning.

"I e-mailed some of the people I work with or have represented—"

"Criminals?" he questioned. "You e-mailed criminals?"

"No, wrongly accused people," she stressed. She refused to take a case unless she believed in the client's innocence. She'd made that abundantly clear and because she kept winning her cases, Eli humored her, saying he saw no reason to tamper with success. "I deal with some very wealthy people."

He thought of the world she was in now. A-list people, people rich enough to buy and sell Hades a thousand times over.

"Must have been a culture shock, coming back here," he imagined.

"Will you let me talk?" she pleaded.

"Sorry." Taking one hand off the steering wheel, he

raised it in a gesture of surrender. "The floor is yours, Irena."

"Thank you." She still talked quickly, knowing he was going to interject something. It was only a matter of time. "Anyway, bottom line is I asked them for contributions."

"Contributions?" He wasn't following her. "For what? You planning on running for office?"

"God, no." No way would she ever consider setting foot in that kind of whirlpool. "But I started thinking how you were going to wind up running out of funds helping these people—"

"My choice," he interjected, not wanting to be on the receiving end of a lecture. "And I get back more than I give."

"Well, now you can give more as well. Or work with more, your choice."

She wasn't making any sense again. He knew that he was completely captivated by her, but right now her thought process left something to be desired. Like illumination.

"What?"

Irena put her hand over his mouth.

When he raised his eyebrows, she told him, "This is the only way I'll be able to finish a sentence." She kept her hand in place and continued her explanation. "I thought if we set up a nonprofit foundation to help the tribe build up their homes, pull their own weight so to speak and assist them in standing up on their own two feet, it might help you accomplish what you set out to do without it completely bankrupting you.

"I also e-mailed the people I went to law school with

whom I still keep in touch. A lot of them have done very well for themselves. I suggested that we might set up a scholarship. You know, nothing huge, just something that might allow for two promising high school graduates to go on to college each year."

Finished, Irena took her hand away from his mouth. Brody merely looked at her.

"Well, say something," she finally implored when the silence threatened to stretched out far beyond a few minutes.

His eyebrows raised in mock wonder. "I can talk now?"

"Yes, you can talk now," she ground out.

He laughed at that. "Too bad, because I'm speechless," he admitted. And then he watched her closely, as if he couldn't quite make himself believe this turn of events. "You really did all this?"

"I sent out the e-mails and outlined the plan in each case—scholarship or foundation—if that's what you mean. And the good news is," she finally got to it, "I received all sorts of pledges back."

"In other words, promises."

She could tell what he thought of promises by the way he said the word. Who had broken a promise to him, she wondered. But then, she realized, he had no reason to believe these promises. After all, they came from people who were her friends, not his. She needed to make him understand.

"These people live up to their word, Brody. And even if they only give half of what they pledged—and they won't, they'll give the entire amount," she assured him, "you'll have a sizable chunk of money to work with." More ideas popped into her brain. "You could even build a clinic on the reservation," she enthused. "Sick people wouldn't have to find a way to drive all the way into Hades for medical attention if they didn't want to."

Brody could remember a time, not all that long ago, when Hades had had only one doctor of their own. It was just after Dr. Shayne's brother, Ben, left town. Now Ben was back and they had not only him and Dr. Shayne, but April's husband, Jimmy, as well. They all worked at the clinic, sometimes hours after the doors were technically closed.

"That would be a vast improvement," he agreed, measuring his words out slowly. He didn't want to allow himself to get carried away. The tribe needed so many things. "You sure these people you contacted can be counted on to back up their donations?"

She was more than sure. "I just set the proposition before them and asked for help. I didn't specify any amounts," she pointed out. "Each person I e-mailed suggested the size of their own contributions." It made her feel good inside because she'd wound up getting far more than she'd initially hoped for.

Brody tried to think logically. If this happened, there were still problems. "Listen, I don't have the knowledge to set up these things." And the closest lawyer was in Anchorage. It was going to be an ordeal, he thought, trying to find someone he trusted. "A foundation, or a scholarship fund," he repeated. "I don't know the first thing about getting—"

Irena cut him off. "That's okay. I do."

He felt adrenaline beginning to pump. He tried his best to sound casual. "Then you are staying?"

If that's what it took, she thought. "Maybe for a little bit," she allowed. Then just in case Farley proved to be immovable, she added, "But I can handle setting them up just as easily from Seattle. This is the age of tele-conferencing," she reminded him. "With a computer and a webcam, I can be anyplace in an instant. Maybe faster."

Speed was not the issue. "True, but having you there instead of here still has its drawbacks."

Had she missed something? Irena thought for a moment. Coming up empty, she asked, "Which are?"

"The fact that an image doesn't feel the same as having you here live and in person." He paused for a moment, knowing if he said this, he would be putting himself out there. But Brody decided to take his chances.

"I can't hold an image in my arms."

His answer made her heart hammer hard and fast.

"Guess not," she murmured. Oh, God, what was she doing, longing for a repeat of the evening in her parents' house? This couldn't go anywhere; she knew that. And still, she heard herself whispering, "Maybe you should be with him while you can."

Brody pulled over his car and turned the engine off. "Are you saying that you'd be willing to go to your house with me tonight instead of back to your grandfather's?"

She knew what he was saying. Or wasn't saying. Irena ran the tip of her tongue along her dry lips. It didn't help. They felt incredibly dry—because the palms of her hands were getting all the moisture in her body. They had suddenly grown damp.

"I am," she said, her voice hoarse.

It took all of Brody's strength not to say the hell with it and drive over to the cabin now. The ache he'd always felt when he thought of her hadn't been alleviated by making love with her the other night. If anything, it had only grown more intense. Because now he knew what he was missing rather than just fantasizing about it.

But there were people waiting for him, people who counted on him and to whom he'd given his word. If he ignored that, then he was no better than those who'd turned their backs on the tribe over the years, ignoring their own consciences—if they had any to begin with.

Even so, as he started up the car again, he began to pray that somehow the day would fly by. And the evening hours wouldn't.

"So tell me more about these donations you extracted," he said to Irena as they drove to the reservation.

When they arrived at the weather-beaten schoolhouse twenty minutes later, they saw that Matthew was already waiting for them, just as he had been the other day. Gathered around Matthew were some of the tribe members. They all seemed rather eager to get started, despite the chill in the air and the gray skies that hovered above them.

As she got out of the car, Irena noted that there were twice as many willing hands as the other day. Not only that but she realized that a number of people from Hades were in the group. Most notably Ike and his cousin.

After exchanging a few words with Matthew, Brody turned toward Ike.

"Looking to pick up some land cheap, Ike?" he asked the other man guardedly. It wasn't that he didn't trust Ike, it was just that these days, everything Ike had an interest in, he wound up owning, either in partnership or outright.

"Looking to spread a little goodwill," Ike corrected. "And give back some of what I've gotten. Behind this handsome exterior," he continued grandly, winking at Irena, "is a man who knows damn well that there but for the grace of God go I." He glanced at his cousin. "Or at least Jean Luc."

"Thanks a lot," Luc deadpanned, pretending to look annoyed.

"It brings balance back to the universe to help those who need it," Ike continued. He pushed up the sleeves of his heavy sweater, exposing muscular forearms. "So, where do we start?"

"C'mon, I'll show you," Brody said. He glanced at Irena, wondering how much she had to do with this, as well. Granted he'd gotten the doctors to come to the reservation once a month, but this was something over and above that effort. The look Irena gave him was one that seemed just a tad too innocent to suit him. But he let it go.

For now.

"You have anything to do with Ike, Jean Luc and the others showing up today?" he asked when, after putting in a full day's work on another new building, they drove to her parents' cabin.

"I came with you, remember?" Irena reminded him. She got out of his car and walked over to the cabin's front door.

He followed her. "That's not answering my question, Irena. You could have gone to Ike yesterday afternoon, asking him to get some volunteers together. Or you could have gotten your grandfather to do it."

She paused, as if considering the idea. "I could have."

Law school had taught her to be tricky, he thought. "Did you?"

She opened the door and walked inside. "Why do you need to know?" she asked. "Isn't it enough that they showed up?"

Turning on the light, Brody shut the door behind him and then flipped the lock, guaranteeing their privacy. "Yes—and no."

"Now you're the one who sounds like a lawyer. Firm but vague," she elaborated with a grin. "You can't have it both ways, Brody." she stripped off her jacket and hung it up. "You have to pick one."

"Then I pick you," she heard him say.

Her back still to him, Irena smiled to herself. Just for now, in this place where she had been just a normal little girl, she could pretend that they were in love. In love and with a future before them. "That wasn't one of the choices."

"Then I want a new game," he told her. "One that has you as a choice." Standing behind her, he slipped his arms around her waist and pulled her closer, nuzzling her. The next moment, he pressed a kiss to the side of her neck.

Irena felt her body instantly heating. Heating from the longing that raced through her, fueled by anticipation and adrenaline. It was hard to think clearly. He made everything slip into a warm haze.

"Don't you want to eat?" she asked with effort.

Some of the women had brought food with them and they'd nibbled as they worked. Food wasn't even remotely on his mind right now.

"I'm looking to obtain my sustenance another way," he told her.

She leaned back into him, the warmth of his body both comforting her and arousing her. She closed her hands around his arms, holding him to her. "Very petty words for a man who works with his hands these days."

"There's a lot to be said for working with your hands." She felt him begin to press his fingertips against her. Her breath began to shorten.

"I didn't say there wasn't."

His breath was warm against her skin. "Would you like a demonstration?"

She wanted to turn around, to kiss him until she couldn't breathe, but she let him lead this time. That was delicious in its own way. "You going to build something for me?"

"Frenzy, I hope." Brody pushed her hair away from the side of her neck and skimmed his lips along her sensitive flesh.

She shivered even as she absorbed the delicious sensation. "Frenzy it is," she breathed, twisting around so that she could face him, her body rubbing against his. Igniting them both.

It was the last thing she said for quite some time to come.

Chapter Twelve

Thanks to a sizable donation from Ike and Jean Luc, the small church had recently been renovated and expanded. Even so, it was filled to capacity, with standing room only as people spilled down the steps and outside the building.

The town of Hades had turned out in force, more to show its support for Brody, whom everyone cared about and admired, than to actually mourn the loss of a man who had never given of himself, except in the most obvious of ways: as a faithless lover.

Irena had arrived early to be there for Brody in any way she could. If her heart still ached a little, it was only in a reflexive capacity. She had laid her feelings for Ryan to rest. Now it was time to do the same with the man.

Sitting in the first pew between Brody and her grandfather, she had turned and looked around the church as people had filed in. Sandwiched in among those strictly there for Ryan were various women, some hardly more than teens, who came to mourn what they felt they'd lost: someone they adored and with whom they had each thought, hoped, to spend the rest of their days.

Ryan had been a charmer to the end, Irena couldn't help but think, watching Ryan's groupies mourn.

And there but for the grace of God go I.

If she hadn't stumbled across Ryan making love with Trisha, who knew how long she would have continued wearing blinders, foolishly believing that she was his "one and only"?

How many of those "one and onlys" had he had during the course of their relationship? Mercifully, she had never gone on to find out. But instinct told her that there had been more than a few. What a fool she'd been, loving him. Thinking that he loved her. Thinking she was one of the luckiest women on earth.

Well, she had been, Irena silently argued. Not because she'd been with Ryan but because she'd managed to walk away. Leaving Ryan and Hades had turned out to be the best thing in the world for her. Without Ryan to cloud her thinking process, she'd gone on to make something of herself, to forge a career. And, in so doing, she was now in a position to give back a little to the region that had once been her home.

As the minister stood at the pulpit, urging them all to "use your time on earth well," she definitely didn't regret loving Ryan. She was just grateful that she'd stopped loving him when she had.

As the minister came to the end of his sermon, signaling that the funeral was almost over, Irena took a deep breath and then let it out.

Hearing her, Brody felt a pang. The next moment, the momentary tinge of jealousy was followed by a wave of guilt. This was his brother's funeral. Ryan was gone and he was alive. He shouldn't be feeling this kind of animosity toward Ryan. And he certainly shouldn't be entertaining any jealousy.

Ryan paid the ultimate price. He was dead by his own hand. The only kind of emotion he should be feeling was pity.

Instead, he was angry at Ryan.

Angry that he had wasted his life this way and even angrier that his brother had managed to hurt so many people during the course of that short life.

Angry that Ryan had managed to hurt the woman beside him, Brody thought. A woman he himself had always loved.

Still loved.

And the sigh he'd just heard escape her lips told him that she still loved Ryan.

Inclining his head toward Irena, Brody whispered, "Are you all right?"

She hadn't meant to sigh. Irena pressed her lips together and nodded.

"I should be asking you that question." She looked at him. "Are you?"

"I'm fine," he assured her.

The minister stepped away from the pulpit. The service was over. People at the back of the church began filing out of the pews, heading toward the open double doors. It was time to go to the cemetery. He slanted another look in Irena's direction.

"You don't have to come if this is upsetting you too much," he told her.

She looked into his eyes for a moment as they rose to their feet. Always thinking of everyone else but himself, she thought. "How is it that you and Ryan share the same DNA?"

Brody shrugged and there was just the hint of a smile on his lips. "Just the magic of science, I guess." And then he became serious. "Really, though, if this is too much for you—"

"Don't worry about it." The sobbing that had continued throughout the service seemed to escalate, as if the person had lost the ability to stop crying. Irena glanced around, then located the source. "Tessa, though, doesn't sound as if she's going to make it. Was she Ryan's latest?" she asked in a barely audible voice, even though she was pretty certain she knew the answer.

He nodded. "One of them, yes." Brody lifted his shoulders in a helpless shrug. "He went on being Ryan right up until the end," he told her quietly.

She'd expected nothing less and felt sorry for the women who had come after her. The women who had been taken in by his charm and guile.

They were outside the church now. She noticed even more people than there had been in church, then realized that Matthew, Ed Fox and some of the others from the reservation had stood outside the crowded building, being part of the service without intruding.

They were here, obviously, for Brody. She sincerely doubted that Ryan had even been aware of the reservation's existence. It was beyond the town's boundaries. Beyond Ryan's comfort zone.

"A lot of people came out for Ryan," Brody was saying.

His words caught her attention. Didn't he realize why so many people were here? That if Brody hadn't been his brother, the only ones who would have attended were the heartbroken women Ryan had left behind?

"They came out for you, Brody, not Ryan," she pointed out.

Brody made no response. Ambivalent feelings ricocheted through him. He mourned the loss of the man his brother could have been and grieved because now Ryan would never be able to reach that plateau.

Ike came up to them and placed a hand on Brody's shoulder. The light of compassion was in his eyes. "It's time, Brody," he said simply.

Brody nodded. Without a word, he turned on his heel. He, Ike, with Jean Luc, Shayne, Ben and Jimmy falling into place, went around the side of the building.

Irena watched them. When she looked back, she caught her grandfather looking at her. She anticipated his question and answered without giving him a chance to ask.

"I'm fine, Grandpa."

Rather than probe, she was surprised to see Yuri nod his head instead.

"I am knowing this," he told her softly. A smile she

couldn't begin to fathom was on his lips. The look in his eyes told her that her grandfather was "knowing" a great deal more than that. Or at least thought he did.

The next moment, Brody and the other five men returned, dividing the weight of the coffin between them as they carried it and slowly made their way to the nearby cemetery.

Irena fell into step directly behind them.

It was as if someone had thrown a switch.

The weather grew colder as they stood gathered around the deep, rectangular hole in the ground and the casket that rested beside it. The minister had selected a short reading from the Bible, the passage that mentioned the body's return to ashes. She really wasn't listening that closely. The sobs coming from several of the women made it difficult to hear.

It was the kind of send-off she knew that Ryan would have appreciated. He always liked being the center of attention, and he particularly liked being the center of attention where women were involved.

She was probably the only one here mourning his lost potential. She and Brody, Irena silently amended, glancing to her left. His profile was rigid, as if he was holding himself in check.

Brody was alone now, and even though he and Ryan could have never been mistaken for two of the musketeers, she knew Brody had to be feeling a sudden emptiness, a deep sense of bereavement.

As the minister finished his reading and closed the Bible he was holding, she slipped her hand into Brody's and gave it a quick squeeze. She continued holding his hand as the casket was secured, then slowly lowered into the ground.

Brody stoically watched the entire process, his expression remaining immobile. Then, when the casket was in the ground and the winches were removed, he picked up a shovel and began to fill the hole.

Silently, one by one, Matthew, Ike and the other pallbearers joined in the effort. It was over with quickly.

Setting his shovel back on the ground, Ike turned to face Brody. "You're coming to the Salty Dog." It wasn't an invitation but a mandate.

Brody shook his head, staring at the fresh mound of dirt. "I don't much feel like celebrating his life, Ike," he told him honestly.

Ike clamped an arm around Brody's shoulders in a bracing gesture. It was obvious that Ike was not about to take no for an answer.

"Then celebrate your own," he suggested. "Lily's catering the food. She's spent all morning preparing different dishes, and believe me, you don't want to say 'No, thank you, I'll pass,' to the woman. Not if you value your head being where it is."

"Amen to that," Alison chimed in with feeling. "My sister gets very testy when it comes to having her food rejected." She turned toward her brother-in-law. "Right, Max?"

The sheriff laughed dryly. "'Fraid so. Better just come peaceably, Brody," he counseled. "If not for yourself, then do it for the town." He punctuated his recommendation with a wink.

Brody didn't answer immediately. He'd wanted to be alone. Alone with his feelings, alone with his memories and, just possibly, alone with Irena for what could be the last time. She still hadn't said anything about staying past tomorrow.

But it looked as if he wasn't about to get the chance to do any of that, especially the latter. Inclining his head, he acquiesced to Max's entreaty, murmuring, "I guess I can't buck the whole town."

Max kept a straight face as he nodded. "No point in even trying."

Hooking her arm through Brody's, Irena flashed a comforting smile at him and started to follow Ike who was leading the way back.

"It'll do you good," she told Brody, lowering her voice because she knew how very private he could be at times.

"Maybe," Brody agreed, trying to sound as if he actually believed what he was saying. Still, he appreciated what everyone was trying to do, appreciated the fact that, as Irena had said, they were all there for him.

Behind him Brody heard more than one woman begin to sob again. The volume seemed to increase. He looked back over his shoulder. Standing over the grave site, Tessa and two other women had dissolved in tears for what seemed like the third time.

Brody stopped walking.

"What's the matter?" Irena asked.

He nodded toward the women. "Someone should go comfort Tessa, Grace and Jill."

The moment he said that, Ike's wife, Marta,

Shayne's wife, Sydney, and Jimmy's wife, April, all three of whom were right behind him, fell back.

"Already taken care of," Marta replied, gesturing for him to continue on to the saloon. Turning, she and the other two women made their way over to the last of Ryan Hayes's women.

Irena watched the six women interact for a moment and smiled to herself. She'd forgotten how well coordinated everyone could be in this tiny after-thought of a town. While it was true that, for the most part, the people who lived here were far from sophisticated, their decency and basic set of values elevated them above a lot of the people she encountered in her incredibly fast-paced day to day life in Seattle.

The wind might have ushered in a chill, she thought, turning back to Brody, but there was an undeniable warmth generated here that no amount of wind could dissipate.

The celebration after Ryan Hayes's funeral went on through the late afternoon and continued long after the sun had gone down, threading into the evening. Because Ike and Jean Luc made a point of running a family oriented saloon, no one had to leave the premises because they had a family waiting for them at home.

Instead, all the family members, from the youngest child to the oldest spouse or grandparent, were right there with them. And, as Ike had pointed out to Brody, the gathering was far more a celebration of life than a mourning of the passing of someone whose life had not touched as many as it should have.

Brody found himself surrounded by friends who were more family to him than his late brother and father had ever been. It made him grateful that he lived where he did.

Still, he thought, he'd give it all up in a heartbeat to be with Irena.

If she asked him to.

He pushed the thought from his mind. No point in entertaining fantasies. He's shared two incredible nights with her, and he would have to be satisfied with that.

It was more than he'd had before.

The din grew louder as more and more people crowded into the saloon and competed with one another, raising their voices in order to be heard.

Irena observed the people around her rather than talked. And, because he was first and foremost a beloved friend, she took it upon herself to make sure that Brody was never left alone for more than a couple of minutes at a time. She sincerely believed that he needed to be kept occupied so that his thoughts, which had to be painful right now, didn't run away with him.

Eventually, the party wound down and the crowd thinned out again. Most of the people who had come from the reservation had said their goodbyes to Brody much earlier. Their exodus was eventually followed by the others.

It was getting late. Time for them to leave, Irena thought. She looked around for Brody. She'd seen him with Max a few minutes ago, but Max had just walked past her and Brody wasn't with him.

She curbed the urge to ask the sheriff if he knew where Brody was. That would make her sound like a mother hen, and she didn't want people getting the wrong idea.

Was it the wrong idea? A small voice in her head asked.

Shutting the voice out, she wandered through the saloon, weaving in and out between people, looking for Brody and trying not to be obvious.

She finally saw him over by the buffet tables that Ike and Jean Luc had set up to hold Lily's food.

As expected, there was nothing left on the plates. Every last morsel was gone. Lily prided herself on the fact that she didn't make the kind of food people stored for another day. Even stuffed to the gills, if there was a bite left, they would consume it. It was what made her restaurant so popular.

Walking up behind Brody, she saw that he wasn't scavenging for food. Instead he was neatly stacking the plates.

"What are you doing?" she asked.

"Cleaning up," Brody answered simply, depositing one stack of plates on a tray. He intended to bring them into the small kitchen in the back and wash them.

"No, you're not," Irena insisted, removing his hands from the dishes. She placed herself between him and the tables. "You're emotionally wrung out, Brody. You're not supposed to do anything except sit around and talk if you feel up to it."

"I've been doing that for—" Brody paused to check his watch "—the last ten hours," he pointed out. He reached for another plate and found his hand deftly blocked by her body. "My jaw hurts, Irena. I need to do something physical."

"Okay," she agreed, taking him by the hand and drawing him away from the tables. "You can come outside and go for a walk with me."

He found himself being led to the front door. "But Lily—"

"Can take care of her own plates," Lily announced, walking past Brody and to the buffet tables. She smiled at him as she did so. "That's why God invented husbands," she assured Brody, beckoning for hers to come over. "To help pick up the slack."

"And for a few other things," Max said with a wicked grin as he joined her.

"And for a few other things," Lily echoed. She paused for a moment to lean into Max, her body language testifying just how very compatible they were. "Now go," Lily ordered Brody, turning her attention back to him. "Leave all this to me. To us," she amended, her eyes meeting Max's.

"Everything was great," Brody told her. He'd nearly forgotten to thank her.

The smile on Lily's face was one of self-satisfaction. "Yes, I know."

Standing behind her, Max wrapped his arms around her waist. "Gotta do something about that overwhelming modesty of yours, Lil."

Very gently, Lily removed his arms and went back to stacking dishes. "I put a lot of effort into being as good as I possibly can," she reminded her husband.

Max lowered his voice and whispered, "I'll remember that tonight."

Max obviously thought his voice was low enough,

but Irena had heard him. She couldn't help envying Lily, she thought, slipping on her parka. Banking down her thoughts, she turned toward Brody.

"C'mon, let's get you out into the fresh air," she said cheerfully.

He could see through her, Brody thought. She was deliberately trying to be cheerful in order to cover up what she was going through. All this domestic harmony and wordplay had probably made her miss Ryan even more.

Irena would always be Ryan's girl, he thought, resigning himself to the fact. He was just fooling himself if he believed anything else.

He gestured toward the door. "After you," he said, profoundly wishing that he didn't ache for her so.

Chapter Thirteen

"Are you going to be all right?" she asked Brody as he pulled his car up in front of Yuri's house later that night.

After leaving the saloon, they had both lost track of time as they'd walked and talked. It had been more than an hour later that they'd finally gotten into his car and driven over to her grandfather's house.

There was a single light shining on the porch, a beacon to guide her home. Now that she was here, she realized that she didn't want to go home. She wanted to remain with Brody.

Was that selfish of her?

Maybe.

She looked at him with concern now, ready to jump at any excuse to stay with him.

He turned off the ignition, then shifted to look at her. The light from the porch helped illuminate the inside of the cab. Her face was bathed in partial shadows. His fingertips itched to lightly trace them.

"Funny," he said, "I was just going to ask you the same question."

Irena shrugged.

"I'm fine, but I was—am—" she corrected herself "—worried about you."

She didn't want him to be alone, he thought. And she didn't realize that he'd been alone long before Ryan had terminated his life.

"Don't be," he assured her. "Except for when I was cleaning up his messes, Ryan and I didn't interact all that much." Brody laughed dryly. "He thought I was wasting my life. I thought he was wasting his." But he'd loved his brother, warts and all. He just hadn't liked him very much. "There wasn't much common ground."

"Wasting your life?" she echoed incredulously. Without consciously realizing it, she wrapped her arms around herself as the chill sliced through the closed car. "By helping others?"

He thought of his brother's vocation: to make love with every breathing, desirable woman he came across. Ryan very nearly succeeded with all the single ones. And more than a couple of the married ones, as well. His brother had had a gift for making women feel special, feel pretty. Until he was tired of them. "Ryan had his own definition of helping others."

"Yes, and very strict requirements regarding *who* he'd help." Again she upbraided herself. She considered herself a fairly intelligent woman. How could she have been so very blind all those years? Or was it just that, subconsciously, she didn't want to know? "They had to be female, young and nubile."

Brody's quiet laugh had no humor in it. "That about sums it up."

Her hand on the car's door handle, she made a move to get out, then stopped. Irena glanced at him. "I don't have to go in if you want to hang out for a little while longer."

Her words, uttered so innocently, tempted him. More than anything, he wanted to take her home with him. Wanted to lose himself in her, not to forget anything, but to remember. Remember the touch, the taste, the scent and feel of her. Because, in the back of his mind, he knew it was going to have to last him a lifetime.

He'd been born pragmatic if nothing else. He couldn't allow his needs to derail her life. "Don't you have a flight to get ready for?" he reminded her.

"Oh, that's right," she recalled suddenly, "I didn't tell you."

Brody's heart, along with his breathing, stopped. He could feel a shaft of light shining through the overwhelming darkness. He did his best to sound normal. "Tell me what?"

Her smile was almost shy, he thought. "That I called Eli today."

The name meant nothing to him. The smile meant everything. "Eli?"

"My boss," she told him, then elaborated further. "Eli Farley is the senior-senior partner. I told him I needed to stay a few extra days in order to get this foundation and the scholarship established. He didn't sound very happy," she admitted, remembering how the man's voice had boomed in her ear as he demanded to know if her extended stay was "absolutely necessary?" "But at bottom," she continued, "he is a generous, decent man." The smile on her lips had filtered into her eyes and was now warming him as he looked at them, mesmerized. "And I reminded him that I do have a ton of days I haven't taken yet. So he finally agreed to give me the extra time off." Her grin grew wider. There was more, he thought. "I also got him to make a contribution."

This time, his laugh was gentle and heartfelt. "You are incredible."

Her eyes crinkled with pleasure. "I like the sound of that."

And he liked the fact that he had her for a little while longer. "So how long are you staying—wait," he said abruptly, changing his mind. "Don't tell me. I'd rather not put a finite point to your visit."

"Not knowing doesn't change anything," she pointed out.

"No," he agreed. It didn't change anything, but it could let him go on pretending. "But humor me."

"Done." Her eyes teased his. "You know what this means, don't you?"

That I've been given a reprieve and can have you in my life a little longer.

Brody was fairly certain that wasn't what she meant, so he said, "Enlighten me."

"It means I can go with you to the reservation on Monday and help put up the next house."

"What about filing the papers?" he reminded her.

She shook her head. "Monday is never a good day to file papers." Experience had taught her that. "Too many people are always competing with one another for court time."

"An extra set of hands is always welcome." He was still struggling not to sound overly enthusiastic or let the burst of happiness get the better of him.

The cold found its way into every corner of the car. They couldn't just sit here like this. Much as he could go on talking to her all night, she should go inside.

"Can I kiss you good-night?" he asked her.

No doubt about it, the man made her pulse race. "I have a better idea."

The gleam in her eyes was seductive. "Oh?"

Slowly, Irena nodded her head. "Take me to your place."

Nothing would have made him happier, but he looked at Yuri's small house with its vigilante porch light. "Won't your grandfather mind you not coming home at a decent hour?"

"It's already too late for that," she pointed out, holding up the wrist with the watch on it. They were swiftly approaching one in the morning. "And as for his 'minding,' my grandfather will probably take out an ad in the newspaper, announcing that you and I have been 'spending time together.' Grandpa thinks you're the best thing to come along since sliced bread." She smiled to herself, thinking how her grandfather would actually react to the idiom. Undoubtedly he would begin asking questions about the bread. "Or he would if he knew what that meant." Brody wasn't restarting the car. Instead, the key was still idly sitting in the ignition. "Something wrong?" she asked. "Why aren't you driving away?"

"If you're doing this for me," he began, then started again. "If the reason you want to come over is that you think that I shouldn't be alone tonight—"

She cut him off. "Maybe I'm the one who shouldn't be alone tonight."

He found that highly suspect. "You said you were fine."

She was. And she wasn't. Irena took in a deep breath. "Don't overthink things, Brody. Just let them be."

She was right. Here he was, fending off exactly what he wanted. What was wrong with him? Brody turned the key in the ignition. The engine came to life. "Words to live by," he agreed.

Even though it was too dark to make out her face once they were driving, he could feel Irena's smile as it curved her mouth.

"I'd forgotten that this looked more like a Swiss chalet than a house," Irena said, standing just inside the threshold as he turned on the lights in his house.

The ceilings were two stories tall, melding into the second floor. There was an open staircase off to one side leading to the bedrooms. The kitchen, dining and living areas were all downstairs, forming one giant communal room.

The last time she'd been here was ten years ago. The memory was not a good one.

"It's really too big for one person," Brody commented, checking the door to make sure it was closed. Turning around he faced her again. "I've been thinking of selling it and building something smaller."

She couldn't picture those words coming out of the mouth of any of the people she knew in Seattle. "Most people aspire to move up, not move down."

"A house doesn't define you," he replied. Going over to the large bay window that looked out on the town, he closed the curtains. There was no point in fueling any gossip. "Besides," he turned back to look at her, "I'm not most people."

"No," she agreed, glancing at the books he had displayed on his bookcase. A wide variety of subjects were covered. She recalled that he'd always had an inquisitive mind. "You certainly aren't."

Brody came up behind her, placing his hands on the sides of her shoulders. Breathing in the light scent of her vanilla and jasmine shampoo.

"So where do we go from here?" he heard himself asking, even though he'd sworn that he wouldn't project past the moment he was in.

"You could light a fire," she suggested, turning around to face him. There it went again, she thought. Her heart was slipping into double-time. When it wasn't skipping a beat. If she were cynical, she would have attributed that to arterial fibrillation. But this wasn't anything that could be found in a medical book. "In the fireplace I mean," she added, a hint of an amused smile playing on her lips.

"A fire in the fireplace it is," he agreed.

Crossing to the hearth, he got busy. He already had the correct combination of hard and soft woods to start his fire and keep it going. Taking the sheets of newspaper he had stacked on the side, he inserted strips in between the logs.

He crouched beside the hearth, took a match and lit the strips. He let the wood do the rest. The flame progressed from the newspaper strips to the pine wood and then, finally, to the oak that comprised the core of his wood.

"Anything else?" he asked, turning his head toward her.

Irena crouched down beside him, pushing her hair away from her face. It was a stall tactic. Her heart was racing, even as common sense told her to bid him a good-night and go home. The night was clear; she could make it back to her grandfather's house without a problem.

She didn't move. Couldn't move.

Brody wasn't the only one playing with fire. She was, too. Moreover, she was playing with the most dangerous kind of fire. The kind that could burn her, leaving indelible marks that no one but she would ever see.

Damn it, she knew better than to live in just the moment. What she was doing went against her carefully crafted life.

And yet, she couldn't seem to help herself. Couldn't make herself leave.

"Surprise me," she told him.

The words, emerging in a soft whisper, seemed to

skim along his cheek, enticing him, stealing away his breath.

Taking her hand, Brody rose to his feet, drawing her up with him.

Without a word, he pressed his lips to hers, taking the first step that would lead him to a night of lovemaking, the way he'd thought about, heaven help him, all during the funeral service and even more so throughout the entire evening at Ike and Jean Luc's saloon.

She was like a fever in his blood and, as with all fevers, he knew there would be a time when the fever would break. But he didn't want to think about that, didn't want even to know when she would leave. That way, he could pretend that she would remain with him forever.

Something that he knew he had absolutely no right to ask her.

He wasn't his brother. And, unlike his brother, he wouldn't take a moment with her for granted. Because he knew it was a gift.

A gift he was going to make the most of.

Passion exploded between them right from the first moment. Brody made love with her on the wide, comfortable sofa that stood facing the fireplace. Then, in a far more traditional manner, he made love with her in his bedroom. Twice.

He made love with Irena as if there was no tomorrow. Because, to him, tomorrow did not exist. There was only now.

Only her.

And that was more than enough.

* * *

It was done.

The papers for both the foundation, which she had insisted bear Brody's name, and the scholarship, to which she had wisely affixed Eli Farley's name in order to please the senior lawyer as well as to secure further contributions from the man, were properly filed at the courthouse in Anchorage. Kevin had flown her there and back himself, refusing to allow her to pay for the flight despite the cost of fuel.

"My contribution," he had told her once they returned to the terminal.

And establishing the two, she thought now, holding copies of the legal papers in her hand, had been hers, along with some of the initial funding. All she had to do was give these copies to Brody and her part in this was done.

Which, she recognized, took away her one concrete excuse for remaining in Hades.

Irena sighed.

She could only put her life in Seattle, her career with the firm, on hold for just so long. Two and a half weeks was really stretching Farley's patience. She had cases waiting for her, he'd reminded her when she'd last called him.

Of course she'd made sure that all the cases were well covered before she ever left, but they were still hers and the clients deserved to have her attention. That was what they were paying for and it was only right.

Still, if she was being honest with herself, she knew that she'd turn her back on her integrity, her cases, her luxurious apartment. Give up everything in a heartbeat, if Brody asked her to.

She'd shared her feelings with June, who'd commented that she didn't look very happy for a woman who had managed to do so much for so many so quickly.

"That doesn't sound very liberated, does it?" she concluded.

June, who'd listened without comment, continued to look at her thoughtfully. "That all depends."

From where she stood, there were no shadings in the situation. "On what?"

"On your game plan," June told her. "On whether or not you want to walk through life alone or beside a good man."

"Before I came back here, I thought it was the former. Now…" Irena's voice trailed off for a moment as she searched her heart—which was in definite conflict with her mind. "I don't know anymore."

June nodded, as if she could see right through her. As if, once upon a time, she'd gone through the same thing herself.

"Does Brody know how you feel?"

Irena laughed softly to herself. "Unless he's completely dense, I'd say yes, he probably knows."

That should have settled it. Ursula had maintained more than once that Brody was smitten with Irena and she knew better than to doubt her grandmother's powers of observation and ability to eavesdrop.

"Then I don't understand," June said. "What's the problem?"

"The problem is he hasn't said anything." It hurt to

even say that, to talk about it. "Hasn't asked me to stay. Not really," she emphasized. Irena began to pace. "I've been the one who made all the first moves and I guess I don't mind that. But there comes a time when a woman wants to know she's wanted. Wants to know that she's not just fooling herself into believing something that isn't true."

"Brody's not Ryan. I really don't remember seeing Brody with another woman—except when he was picking up the pieces that Ryan left behind."

Irena put the legal papers aside before she wound up twisting them apart. "That's just it. I don't want to be just another woman whose pieces he's picking up out of the goodness of his heart."

June turned a chair around and sat down, facing Irena. "Well, as an outside observer, I don't think you are."

Irena stopped pacing. "Then why hasn't he come right out and asked me to stay?"

"I don't know. Hey, here's a novel idea. Why don't you ask him?"

Definitely a bad idea. Irena shook her head. "No, I can't just put myself out there like that."

"But—"

On this she was firm. He had to come to her, say something to her. She couldn't be the one who spoke up first. "I wouldn't be able to stand it if he tells me that he doesn't care one way or the other."

"And if he says he does care? If he asks you to stay?" June pressed.

"I still won't know if he means it, or if he just said

that because he doesn't want to hurt my feelings." She sighed, shoving her hands into the back pockets of her jeans. "I guess it's a no-win situation."

"Do you love him, Irena?" June asked quietly.

Irena didn't want to say the words out loud. Because then she couldn't take them back. What she was feeling would have a name, a label. It would be real.

She shrugged, looking off. "I don't know. Maybe I just think I do. Maybe coming back here for Ryan's funeral just raised too many memories, stirred up too many old feelings to deal with. Maybe—"

"Maybe you've been a lawyer too long," June interjected, "and you've forgotten how to give a straight answer. Do you love him?" she repeated. "C'mon, Irena. Yes or no?"

Irena took in a breath and then let it out again. It sounded shaky to her ear. As was she.

"Yes," she replied softly. "I do. And it doesn't change a damn thing." And then she suddenly turned around and looked at June. "And you're not to say anything to him, do you hear me? You have to promise me that you won't tell Brody—or Ursula—what I just said."

"All right," June replied, rolling her eyes. "I promise I won't tell Brody—or my grandmother," she added as Irena pinned her with a look, "what you just said."

June never lied, Irena thought. She knew that. But for some reason, she still didn't feel comforted by her promise.

Chapter Fourteen

Irena watched as Brody walked into the Salty Dog Saloon and sat down at the bar beside her. Even then, after exchanging a few words in greeting, she searched for the right way to tell him. She hoped he would say what she wanted him to say.

But there were no magical words. She just had to spit it out. Looking into her ginger ale, Irena said, "I'm leaving tomorrow."

Brody didn't move a muscle and there was no inflection in his voice, no surprise, no disappointment. Nothing. Only a single word of acknowledgment. "Oh."

Stung, she couldn't help but ask, "Don't you have anything to say?"

He half turned to look at her. She was ripping out his heart. What more did she want from him? "Goodbye?"

"That's it?" she asked incredulously. "That's all?"

"Good luck?" he suggested. It was all he could do to hold himself together. He didn't want her to leave, but if she stayed, he knew it wasn't because of him she was staying. It was because he reminded her of Ryan. "What is it you want me to say?" he asked.

What did he want? Cue cards? Was he that dense, or was he like Ryan after all?

"Nothing you want to say?" She sighed, shaking her head. "I can't put words into your mouth." She replayed the last sentence and amended it. "I don't *want* to put words into your mouth."

And apparently, you can't think of any on your own that I desperately want to hear.

How many times was she going to have to put herself out there before she learned her lesson? Before she finally surrendered and acknowledged that love just wasn't for her?

Irena closed her eyes, as if that could somehow contain her pain, keep it under wraps.

"Anyway, I just wanted you to know." Opening her eyes, she pushed the large manila envelope on the bar toward him. "Here are all the papers for the foundation and the scholarship. They've all been properly filed in Anchorage."

He stared at the envelope, not really seeing it. Seeing, instead, how empty his life was going to be with her gone.

But in these last three weeks that she'd been here, a

real, tangible part of his world, he'd discovered something about himself. That he did love her to almost the point of distraction but that, no matter what he'd originally thought, he *wasn't* up to accepting Ryan's table scraps. Certainly not up to competing with his brother's memory. He didn't want to be a substitute for Ryan; he wanted Irena to love him for himself.

And that wasn't about to happen. He looked too much like his brother to delude himself.

Brody drummed his fingers over the envelope. "I don't know the first thing about what to do with all this," he told her.

She waited a moment. Waited for more to follow. It didn't. Disappointment took bitter, sharp chunks out of her. Brody couldn't even ask her to stay to help him with that.

"I talked to Ike." She nodded toward the man who was drying glasses on the far end of the bar. Ike nodded back but remained where he was, as if sensing that his absence was preferable. "He's pretty savvy when it comes to this sort of thing. He'll help you through it if you run into any stumbling blocks."

Brody merely nodded, avoiding her eyes. "Good to know," he murmured.

Ask me to stay, you jerk. Tell me you love me, that you can't face tomorrow without me. Make me an offer, any kind of offer. I won't turn you down, she silently pleaded.

But when Brody spoke, it wasn't anything that she wanted to hear.

"Well, take care of yourself, Irena," he told her.

"Don't let it be another ten years before you come back for a visit." Finally turning toward her, he gave her a quick, almost awkward hug, like a boy forced to submit to the ordeal of hugging an overbearing great-aunt.

It left her stunned. This wasn't her lover. It wasn't her friend. This was a stranger. "You're leaving?" she asked shocked.

He picked up the envelope and tucked it under his arm. "Got things to do," he told her. "And so do you, I imagine. There's packing and saying your goodbyes," he added as if she'd asked him what it was that he thought she had to do.

"Right. Packing and saying goodbye," she repeated, her voice completely devoid of any emotion. It was either that, or exploding at him and she suddenly felt far too drained to do that.

She hadn't realized until this moment that she could feel so devastated again. Could feel so hurt to discover that her leaving seemed to mean nothing to him. All right, she hadn't expected Brody to exactly tear up and beg her to stay, but she'd hoped that telling him she'd decided to leave would have gotten a stronger reaction from him than if she'd proposed he'd change his socks.

Numbed, she watched Brody's back as he walked through the saloon and then out the front door. It swung closed again, shutting out the sunlight.

He was gone, really gone.

Idiot!

Irena wasn't sure who she was addressing, Brody or herself. All she knew was that she needed to blot out this devastating numbness cascading through her, claiming every last inch of her soul.

She raised her hand to catch Ike's attention. "Whiskey, please, Ike," she called out.

In a fluid motion, Ike made his way over to her. He picked up a pint bottle and placed it on the counter before her. "I don't think it's whiskey you'll be needing, darlin'," he told her.

She looked at what he'd brought her. Orange juice. Terrific. She was miserable, but she'd be healthy.

"What I need," she told him, pausing to open the top and then taking a long sip from the bottle, "is to have my head examined."

"We all feel like that sometimes," he allowed amiably.

She raised her eyes to his. There was no judgment in his. "Doesn't make it any better."

"No," he agreed, "it doesn't."

She'd had enough of being healthy. Irena placed the bottle back on the counter and dug into the pocket of her jeans. She took out a five-dollar bill, placing it out the counter between them.

Using two fingertips, Ike pushed it back to her. "Your money's no good here, darlin'."

Her back stiffened. "I can pay for orange juice," she retorted.

His manner never changed. "So can I."

Chagrined at her behavior, Irena pressed her lips together. "I'm sorry," she apologized, "I didn't mean to snap."

"Sure you did. Just not at me," Ike observed. When

she made no comment, he continued cautiously, "Seems to me that you and Brody have been spending a lot of time together these last few weeks."

She raised her eyes to his, instantly defensive. "So?"

"So," he went on mildly, "you'd think that with all that time logged in, the two of you could have had at least one intelligent conversation about your feelings."

Not him, too. First June, now Ike. She was in no state to get into this now. "You don't know what you're talking about, Ike."

"Have it your way," he answered, his tone telling her that he took no offense at her tone or her accusation. "But just for the record, I wasn't born married."

She looked at him quizzically, confused. "What does that have to do with it?"

"I know what it means to be defensive, to try *not* to admit to having feelings for someone because you're so sure it's all one-sided."

"I don't need a father confessor, Ike—or a bartender—this time," she informed him, then added in a softer voice, "What I need is a friend."

"That, darlin', you've always had. It goes without saying," Ike assured her with a wink. "Do you need this 'friend' for anything specific?"

"Look after Brody," she requested. "And if he needs any help with the foundation or the scholarship funding, could you just look over his shoulder and steer him in the right direction?"

"Sure, I could do that. But you could do it a lot better than I could," he reminded her, "seeing as how you set them both up, and you're a lawyer and all."

"Doesn't matter," she murmured. "He didn't ask me to."

Ike studied her for a long moment. "And that would be all it'd take?" he wanted to know. "You'd stay if he asked you to?"

Red flags instantly went up in her head. Was that a gleam she saw in his eye? "Whatever you're thinking of doing, Ike, don't," she cautioned him.

He was the soul of innocence. "What makes you think I'm thinking of doing anything?"

She wasn't taken in for a minute. She didn't need a six-foot cupid behind the scenes, orchestrating things. "I'm serious, Ike. No prodding, no hints, no nothing, do you understand? I do *not* want you saying anything to Brody."

The innocent look was tempered with amusement. "Not even hi?"

She wasn't in the mood to be teased. "You know what I mean."

"Yes, I know what you mean." He grew a little serious. "And it makes me glad that I'm not as young as you are anymore."

"Glad I serve a purpose," she murmured just before she slid off the stool. "Well, take care of yourself, Ike."

He looked at her in surprise. "You sound as if you're going now."

She'd made up her mind. Farley had been after her to return as soon as possible, and now she had no reason not to. "I am."

He seemed a little confused. "I thought you said you were leaving tomorrow." And then, because they both knew he'd been too far away in order to eavesdrop on her conversation with Brody, he grinned and pointed to the mirror. "I saw your lips."

Irena raised her eyebrows. "You read lips?"

"Helps in a noisy saloon," he explained. "Beats saying 'what?' every two minutes."

She supposed he had a point. In any case, it had no effect on her decision. "I might as well go today," she said. "I've done everything I came here to do."

Ike's expression bore doubt. But it didn't matter what he thought. She just wanted to go back to Seattle. And away from here.

"At least let us throw you a party," Ike urged.

"You've already thrown me a party," Irena reminded him.

"A farewell party this time," he clarified.

She shook her head. "I'd rather just say my goodbyes quietly, but thanks anyway."

Ike folded the cloth he was using to wipe down the bar and put it down.

"Sure, don't mention it. Anytime I can *not* throw you a party, just let me know." Coming around the bar, he gave her a long hug. "Take care of yourself, Irena Yovich. And try not to be such a stranger," he instructed. "Come see us once in a while." Releasing her, he took a step back. "It'll do us all some good."

She could argue that point. But instead, she said nothing. She merely nodded her head, doing her best not to cry.

Irena had never fully realized just how lonely a city Seattle could be until she returned to it.

Loneliness seemed to come at her from every angle, covering her with a blanket of darkness.

It was as if there was an abyss inside of her and no amount of noise, of interaction with her colleagues and acquaintances or even burning the midnight oil seemed to fill the gaping emptiness.

She'd never felt this lonely before. This painfully adrift even as she was literally in the middle of chaos. Instead of being well handled the way she'd assumed, her caseload had piled up.

She just had to work harder, Irene silently insisted. Even though she wasn't sure if that was humanly possible, she was fairly certain Eli Farley shared this opinion with her. The senior partner had indicated more than once that he felt no one in his firm could *ever* work too hard.

Well, she was already working at maximum capacity, she realized. Even so, she didn't seem able to get back into the groove she'd vacated to go to Hades.

How long was it going to take?

It had been two weeks since she'd returned. Two weeks in which she'd secretly waited, hoped, *prayed* Brody would get in contact with her. To tell her simply that he missed her. Or to call on some pretext just so that he could hear the sound of her voice.

God knows she'd entertained thoughts of doing that very same thing herself. Only the desire to salvage a tiny piece of her pride had restrained her. But rather than it getting easier as time passed, it was getting progressively harder.

Or, at least it felt that way, she thought, filing into

the tenth floor conference room with the other attorneys of Farley & Roberson.

It was nine a.m. on Monday morning, which meant time for their weekly meeting. They were required to give progress reports, to go over the cases pending and to review and make decisions regarding new cases. The latter had to be examined, and then they would decide whether or not the new cases would be taken on.

Eli Farley and Drew Roberson, the firm's other senior partner, were the last word on every decision, with Farley's opinion ultimately outweighing Roberson's since the latter had a year less with the firm. But as it was, the two rarely disagreed.

The new cases were handed out to the junior attorneys who had to summarize them and weigh the advantages of pursuing them. And whether they could be won. A loss at any level, by even the newest attorney, could reflect badly on them all.

She was up second this morning. She had all her notes in order and spread out in front of her. It had taken her twice as long to compile her report, not because she couldn't obtain the necessary information but because even armed with a slew of information, she just couldn't seem to concentrate.

Words would swim in front of her as if she waded through a sea of alphabet soup rather than try to read a detailed report. Over and over again she found her mind drifting, forcing her to refocus and start from the beginning.

This couldn't continue, she silently told herself. *Get with the program, Irena. He doesn't love you. Don't sacrifice your career for another man who doesn't love you.*

As George Donnelly, an attorney she'd worked with more than once, wrapped up his recommendation on a case involving a high-ranking CEO being sued by his mistress, Irena felt her cell phone vibrate in her jacket pocket. She'd forgotten to turn it off.

Slipping the phone out to remedy that, she couldn't help but glance down to see who was calling. The area code identified it as coming from Alaska.

Whoever it was, she'd call them back after the meeting. Flipping open the phone to shut it off, she saw the text message. Words were moving across the tiny screen, approximating an old-fashioned ticker tape.

As she read, her breath caught in her throat. She couldn't take her eyes off the screen.

"Earthquake hit in a.m. Cave-in at mine. Brody among missing."

The message started again, as if taunting her.

"Something you'd like to share with the class, Irena?" Eli Farley asked sarcastically, his voice breaking through her thoughts.

She looked up at him, stunned. She had to get out of here. She needed to go back. She couldn't just stay here, listening to the junior attorneys drone on as if nothing was happening. Couldn't sit here listening to Eli Farley prattle about prestige.

The next second, to Farley's surprise, she was on her feet. "Yes," she answered with finality. "I have to leave."

She heard Farley calling after her, demanding to know where she was going and why, but she didn't stop to answer. She didn't have time. A dire sense of urgency filled her.

All she could think of was that Brody was buried in a cave-in and that he needed her. She refused to think beyond that or even attempt to follow the situation to a possible dark conclusion.

Brody needed her and she was going. Nothing else mattered.

Chapter Fifteen

All the way to the airport, sitting on the edge of her seat in the back of the taxi like a spring that had been wound too tightly, Irena could only think of getting to Hades.

Now.

No way could she remain here, relying on information relayed to her by various news channels.

What made it all even worse was that there was no longer any phone service, cellular or standard, in Hades. Over and over again she tried to reach someone— *anyone*—who could tell her what was going on.

Every number she tried yielded the same results. Nothing. The quake had been centered fifty miles away from Hades, and while the perky woman on TV announced that there were reports of minimal damage so far, that was only because the center of the 6.4 quake had been in a desolate area.

There was no telling what was happening in Hades.

Irena could recall experiencing earthquakes while she lived there—some minor, some not so minor. Like the one that had taken her father from her. Morgan Yovich had been buried in a mine cave-in for more than a week before rescuers could finally dig him and the men buried with him out. There had been no survivors.

What was Brody doing in the mines? she wondered for the thousandth time. He wasn't a miner; he didn't belong there. He spent his time on the reservation, rebuilding it. What could have drawn him away to go underground? It didn't make any sense. Maybe June had gotten it wrong when she'd sent her the message.

At least she could hope.

It didn't help.

She couldn't find a way to escape the uneasiness. Something was wrong. She could *feel* it, feel it knotting up the pit of her stomach, and she knew that she wouldn't have any peace until she got to Hades. She needed to assess what was happening for herself.

To do that, she needed to get a flight out. Immediately.

Easier said than done.

At first, the impeccably groomed woman at the ticket counter told her that the earliest flight she could get to Anchorage wasn't until the next day, at noon. But the reservation clerk took pity on her after she'd pleaded with the woman, saying her fiancé was doing volunteer work at the epicenter of the quake and she hadn't been able to get in contact with him. The woman finally managed to arrange a flight for her with a different airline located in the next terminal.

Irena had fifteen minutes to pay for her ticket and get over there.

She ran all the way, silently asking God to forgive her for the lie she'd just told. Brody wasn't her fiancé, but the thick-headed idiot could have been, if he'd only asked her to marry him the way he was supposed to. Or at least asked her to stay in Hades with him. She was certain that things could have worked out for them eventually.

Instead, she was down here in Seattle, going through the motions of having a life, pretending that she was getting over him. Knowing deep down that she wasn't and probably wouldn't for a very long time.

She was the last one at the gate. The airline attendant was just about to close it off when Irena came racing past the ticket clerk, gasping for breath and waving her ticket so that the attendant would know why a breathless blonde was charging at him.

"Almost missed your flight," the attendant commented with an amused chuckle, standing to the side in order to let her pass.

"Almost," she gasped in agreement. Hopefully, she wouldn't discover when she finally got to Hades that she had also missed something else.

Let him be alive, she prayed.

She still couldn't get through.

No matter how many different numbers she tried, her

grandfather's, Kevin and June's, Brody's, Ursula at the post office, Max, there was no answer. Hades was as cut off from the world now as it had been more than a hundred years ago.

Progress could only be appreciated when it was suddenly absent. She snapped her cell phone closed.

Picking up her small bag, she hurried off the plane and into the terminal. She didn't stop moving until she reached the area where, less than two months ago, June had met her with the passenger plane.

The area was conspicuously empty.

Not a good sign, Irena thought, trying not to panic. There could be lots of reasons why none of Kevin and June's planes were there. And she certainly hadn't expected Shayne's plane to be there. As one of Hades's three doctors, Dr. Shayne Kerrigan and his wife, Sydney, had to have their hands full right now. Everyone at the clinic probably did.

Irena looked around.

So near and yet so far.

She never truly appreciated the meaning of that old saying until just now. Banking down frustration, she went back into the terminal in search of some kind of transportation.

It took her over an hour, but she finally located someone to take her to Hades. The pilot, retired Air Force Captain Seth Adams, had overheard her asking the clerk at the ticket counter if she knew of anyone willing to take her to Hades, and he had volunteered his services.

"My plane goes where I want her to," he told Irena. "Linda, my ex-wife, never did."

She did her best to look as if she was interested in his story. All she wanted to do was to get to Hades as quickly as possible.

"I don't have much cash on me," she told him once he'd agreed to take her. "But I can write you a check." The man didn't know her from Adam. He might not trust her, she thought. "Or I can try to find an ATM machine if you'd rather have cash."

Seth waved away the offer. "I was going up anyway. Now I've got a direction."

Yes, Virginia, there is a Santa Claus!

She could have hugged him if she wasn't afraid of scaring him away.

They took off right after Seth filed his flight plan with the tower.

From the air, everything seemed fine, Irena looked down at the town as they approached Kevin and June's small airstrip.

It was only as they got closer that she saw how the front of the church had fallen to rubble. Some of the other buildings around it had sustained damages as well while others were untouched. The ravages of the earthquake had been capricious.

And then her attention was drawn to something else.

The takeoff in Anchorage had been bumpy. The landing now was even bumpier, although Seth apparently expected more turbulence. He appeared incredibly pleased with himself as the two-seater stopped taxiing and came to a teeth-jarring halt at the end of the airstrip.

"That was one of Eunice's smoother landings," he told her with pride. "Almost smooth as silk."

"Silk," she echoed numbly. Her hand shook a little as she unbuckled herself. But Adams had gotten her here. If not for him and his wobbly Cessna, she would have still been in Anchorage, begging someone for a ride. "Thank you. Thank you so much."

"Anything I can do?" he asked her as she opened the cabin door.

"If you're good at praying, you might want to say a few for the miners," she tossed over her shoulder.

He nodded a shaggy grey head. "I can do that," he agreed amiably. "But the big guy upstairs doesn't always listen," he warned.

She raised a hand over her head and waved without a backward glance.

Where was everyone?

She wanted to find out if there was any news, and she fervently hoped she could get it from Kevin or June, but neither was in the terminal.

Irena circled the small building, searching for signs of life. She finally found Kevin, who was just getting into his Jeep.

When he saw her, he seemed stunned. "I thought you were in Seattle."

"I was. Five hours ago." She took a breath, bracing herself. "How bad is it?"

"It's not good," Kevin told her honestly. "I was just closing up so I could go join the rescue effort."

Thank God she'd gotten here now instead of later. "Mind if I hitch a ride with you?"

"Sure." He opened the passenger door for her. "Hop in."

She tossed in her bag and then sat down. "Aren't they starting rescue efforts rather late?" she asked. "The last time Hades was hit hard with a quake, there was a rescue party organized within an hour after it hit. Any reason for the delay?" She tried to sound nonchalant even as she dreaded hearing what might be the answer.

"There's no delay," he told her, starting his vehicle. "This is the *second* rescue effort."

"The second one? What happened to the first one?" She had a sinking feeling she already knew but she held out hope.

"There was an aftershock, bigger than the original quake," he said slowly, slanting a glance at her as he drove to the opposite end of the town. "The rescue party was trapped."

She had her answer to what Brody was doing in the mine. He was one of the rescuers. "How many men?"

"In the rescue party? Over a dozen. That makes thirty-two who are still missing. A few managed to run out between cave-ins."

"Who?" she forced herself to ask, her breath evaporating in her throat.

Kevin went down the list of miners, getting to the names of the rescuers last.

Brody's name echoed in her head before Kevin even said it. Her hands turned icy even as a shaft of heat shot through her.

He wasn't dead. He wasn't.

"How long have they been in there?" she finally forced herself to ask.

"The cave-in happened seven hours ago. The aftershock hit a little more than an hour after that." He spared her another, longer glance. "Don't worry, Irena, we'll find him. Want me to drop you off at your grandfather's house?"

"No." As relieved as she was that her grandfather was all right, being at the house rather than at the mine was unthinkable. It was as useless as remaining in Seattle.

"You could stay with June," was Kevin's next suggestion.

She shook her head. Nothing was going to keep her away. "I'm coming with you. To the mine," she added.

"You'll probably just wind up standing around and waiting for hours to hear something—if then."

She had no intentions of standing around. "I'm going to join in the rescue effort," she told him. She saw the skeptical expression in his eyes. "There's got to be something I can do," she insisted. "Swing a pickax, something. I'll dig with my bare hands if I have to."

"I'm sure it hasn't come to that," Kevin said, trying to reassure her.

The moment they got there, Irena leaped out of the truck. As soon as her feet hit the ground, she scanned the area, trying to locate a friendly face, someone to steer her in the right direction.

The second rescue party was organized by Max. The owner of the mine was going over the mine's structural integrity, such as it was, and the possible dangers that were ahead of the men. Both Max and the owner appeared doubtful when she walked up to them and offered to help.

"Maybe you could help Lily with the food," Max suggested gently. "She's been out here, feeding the workers and their families. I'm sure she'd welcome more helping hands."

"As important as that is, Sheriff, no. I'm going with you." Reading his mind, she told him, "I'm a lot stronger than I look," and then she added with more passion than she'd intended. "My father was killed in a cave-in, Max. And I'll be damned if I let that mine take someone else from me."

Without a word, Max handed her a pickax.

Irena blinked back tears, rubbing them away with the back of her hand. "Thanks."

"Just be careful where you swing that thing," he warned. Pointing, he indicated a section to the far left. "We're clearing off an area so we can light a charge."

"Dynamite?" she cried, stunned. That could set off another cave-in. The people trapped inside couldn't take it.

The situation they faced was a grave one. "The miners are running out of air, and we need to get another shaft going so that we can reach them before that happens." Max looked at the faces of the other volunteers who were now gathering around him. "Anyone who knows any prayers, now's the time to say 'em."

Irena was already doing just that.

Fear drove her far beyond what she thought she was capable of. She swung the pickax and dug with her hands as she'd threatened when the rocks could be moved no other way.

And when it came time to light the fuse for the dynamite, her prayers grew more frantic.

Everything felt as if it was moving in slow motion. And then it came. The explosion. It echoed in her brain long after the smoke and actual noise had died down.

It took another hour before they found out if they'd been successful—or if the blast had sealed off the miners and their rescuers permanently.

When the first miner, ashen faced and guided by one of the second wave of rescuers Max had led into the mine, emerged from the cave, she was too numb to join in the cheers that broke out. But Irena felt her cheeks growing damp and knew she was crying.

One by one, the miners and the original men who had gone in to get them came out, straggling, gasping, in some cases badly injured. Twenty-three in all came out.

Brody wasn't one of them.

Nine men still unaccounted for.

Trying not to think of anything but putting one foot in front of the other, Irena hurried over to the last man to come out. One of the original rescuers.

"Herb," she cried, clamping her hand on the man's shoulder to keep him in place, "where are the others?"

He looked dazed, as if he didn't recognize her for a moment.

"They're dead," he finally said, his voice hoarse. The thirty-two-year-old clerk from the Emporium was clearly shaken. "All dead. We were together when it hit." He seemed haunted as he repeated the words. "They're all dead."

Irena refused to believe him. Refused to accept the idea that there were no more survivors coming out of the mine.

"No," she cried.

"All dead," Herb said again just before he began coughing and choking. Jimmy took charge of the man, leading Herb to the makeshift triage tent.

He wasn't dead. He wasn't dead.

Strong arms caught her as Irena rushed to the mouth of the new opening. She was only vaguely aware that it was Ben, Shayne's brother and one of the three doctors on the site, who was holding on to her waist. Keeping her from running inside and looking for Brody.

"You can't go in there," he told her firmly.

Catching Ben off guard, she managed to shrug out of his hold. "The hell I can't," she cried.

But before she could duck into the cave, Max came out. He was covered with dust from his head down to the toes of his boots. As was the man he was half dragging, half carrying out.

"Brody!" she screamed. The next second, she was wrapping her arms around him, holding him up.

Brody blinked, then turned his face toward Max. "Am I dead?" he asked.

"Not unless I am, too," Max told him. He filled his lungs with fresh air. "And I'm not ready to be dead yet, so, no, you're not."

Then he had another question. "What are you doing here?" Brody asked, his words emerging slowly.

"Trying to find you." She choked back a sob. He was

alive. She knew he couldn't have been dead. She struggled not to cry. "You can't be trusted on your own."

This time, his voice a little steadier, Brody turned toward Max again. "I'm really not imagining this?"

Max allowed himself a smile. "Nope."

Drawn by the shouts, Shayne emerged out of the triage tent. "Bring him over here," he called out to Max. "I need to check him out."

Max didn't bother suppressing a laugh. "I think Irena's already doing that."

"I'm serious, Max," Shayne told him. "Get him over here."

Before Max could comply, Irena angled her shoulder beneath Brody's arm, offering her support. Between her and Max, they brought Brody over to the triage tent.

"I can walk, you know," Brody protested.

"Sure you can," Max answered, humoring him. "We just need the exercise."

Brody looked at Irena. "Why did you come?" he asked again.

There was no point in holding back any longer. "I heard about the earthquake," she told him. "And then June sent me a text saying that you were in the mine when it caved in. I couldn't just sit in a courtroom, waiting to hear if you were dead or alive."

Brody half nodded at the answer. "Saves me a trip," he murmured.

"Put him down here," Shayne instructed. There were a handful of cots hastily set up beneath the huge tent.

Both the narrow cots and the tent had come from the Emporium and were actually intended for campers.

Brody winced as Max and Irena eased him onto the closest cot. Shayne began to examine him, but Brody waved him back. "Just give me a minute, please, Doc. I want to finish," he requested.

"Finish what?" Irena didn't know whether to throw her arms around him because he was all right or hit him upside his head for putting her through this kind of anguish. Why did *he* always have to be the hero?

Brody took a shallow breath, trying to work past the pain. His words came out slowly. "I was about to come down to see you when the quake hit," he told her.

Just because she'd hopped on the first flight here and most likely killed her career doing it didn't mean she was stupid. "Right."

"No, really," Brody insisted, taking her hand. Even that movement cost him. It took everything he had not to suck in his breath as another shaft of pain skewered him. "I've got a plane ticket in my pocket." Pain shot up and down his body as he reached into his pocket.

She didn't believe him, but it didn't matter. All that mattered was that Brody was alive.

"You trying to get this?" Max asked, pulling something out of his back pocket.

It was a torn airline ticket.

Irena stared at it, stunned. He was telling the truth. "You were really coming to see me."

Brody started to say something, but a coughing fit cut his words short. He clutched at his side.

"I need to get you to a hospital," Shayne told him

sternly, gingerly touching Brody's side. "I think you've got a cracked rib. Maybe several."

"Not yet," Brody insisted.

"Brody, please. You need to listen to him," Irena told him.

Brody raised his eyes to hers. "I will if you marry me."

Okay, her hearing had just short-circuited. "What?"

"That was why I was coming to Seattle." Each word was torture for him but he had to make her understand. "To tell you I shouldn't have let you go. That I don't care if you're only with me because I remind you of Ryan. I love you, and I'll take you any way I can."

Now she was not only stunned but angry as well. "Is that what you think? That I was with you because you reminded me of Ryan?"

Brody pressed his hand to his side, as if to contain the pain. "Well, weren't you?"

"No, you idiot," she exploded. "And it's not your rib that's cracked if you believe that, it's your head. You're nothing like Ryan. And if I love you, it's *despite* the fact that your face reminds me of Ryan, not because of it."

He heard only one thing. "You love me?"

She backtracked, aware that all eyes had now turned toward them. "I said 'if' I love you." And then she caved. "Oh, hell, yes. Yes, I love you."

"Why didn't you tell me?" he demanded. So much time could have been saved, so much anguish, if he'd only known.

"Why didn't you tell me?" she countered.

"This is all very touching," Shayne interjected, "but you need to get to the hospital, Brody. Sydney's going to be taking three patients to Anchorage Regional Hospital." Shayne glanced over toward Kevin, who was helping Ben with another injured rescuer. "Kevin?"

"I can take at least five," Kevin responded.

Shayne nodded. "All right, we'll send them in order of need. I think that Mr. Romance here can safely wait until the second wave."

Brody smiled, staring at Irena. Half an hour ago, he was pretty certain he was a dead man. Now he had everything to live for. "I think I can find something to do while I wait."

"Whatever you're planning on doing, it'll have to be done gently," she cautioned, afraid that Brody would hurt himself further if he tried to do anything except just sit there. "Very gently."

And the last two words, Irena felt certain as she lightly touched her lips to Brody's, would do justice to describing the rest of their lives together.

As she allowed herself to sink into the kiss, Irena knew she'd finally come home.

* * * * *

Don't miss Marie Ferrarella's next
Special Edition romance,
THE THIRTY-NINE-YEAR-OLD VIRGIN,
available July 2009.

Celebrate 60 years of pure
reading pleasure with Harlequin®!

Harlequin Presents® is proud to introduce
its gripping new miniseries,
THE ROYAL HOUSE OF KAREDES.
An exquisite coronation diamond, split as a symbol
of a warring royal family's feud, is missing!
But whoever reunites the diamond halves
will rule all....

Welcome to eight brand-new titles that unfold
to reveal the stories of kings and queens,
princes and princesses torn apart by pride
and power, but finally reunited by love.

Step into the world of Karedes with
BILLIONAIRE PRINCE, PREGNANT MISTRESS
Available July 2009
from Harlequin Presents®.

ALEXANDROS KAREDES, SNOW DUSTING the shoulders of his leather jacket and glittering like jewels in his dark hair, stood at the door. Maria felt the blood drain from her head.

"Good evening, Ms. Santos."

His voice was as she remembered it. Deep. Husky. Perfect English, but with the faintest hint of a Greek accent. And cold, as cold as it had been that awful morning she would never forget, when he'd accused her of horrible things, called her terrible names....

"Aren't you going to ask me in?"

She fought for composure. Last time they'd faced each other, they'd been on his turf. Now they were on hers. She was in command here, and that meant everything.

"There's a sign on the door downstairs," she said, her tone every bit as frigid as his. "It says, 'No soliciting or vagrants.'"

His lips drew back in a wolfish grin. "Very amusing."

"What do you want, Prince Alexandros?"

A tight smile eased across his mouth and it killed her that even now, knowing he was a vicious, arrogant man, she couldn't help but notice what a handsome mouth it was. Chiseled. Generous. Beautiful, like the rest of him, which made him living proof that beauty could, indeed, be only skin deep.

"Such formality, Maria. You were hardly so proper the last time we were together."

She knew his choice of words was deliberate. She felt her face heat; she couldn't help that but she damned well didn't have to let him lure her into a verbal sparring match.

"I'll ask you once more, your highness. What do you want?"

"Ask me in and I'll tell you."

"I have no intention of asking you in. Tell me why you're here or don't. It's your choice, just as it will be my choice to shut the door in your face."

He laughed. It infuriated her but she could hardly blame him. He was tall—six two, six three—and though he stood with one shoulder leaning against the door frame, hands tucked casually into the pockets of the jacket, his pose was deceptive. He was strong, with the leanly muscled body of a well-trained athlete.

She remembered his body with painful clarity. The feel of him under her hands. The power of him moving over her. The taste of him on her tongue.

Suddenly, he straightened, his laughter gone. "I have not come this distance to stand in your doorway," he said coldly, "and I am not going to leave until I am ready to do so. I suggest you stand aside and stop behaving like a petulant child."

A petulant child? Was that what he thought? This man who had spent hours making love to her and had then accused her of—of trading her body for profit?

Except it had not been love, it had been sex. And the sooner she got rid of him, the better.

She let go of the doorknob and stepped aside. "You have five minutes."

He strolled past her, bringing cold air and the scent of the night with him. She swung toward him, arms folded. He reached past her, pushed the door closed, then folded his arms, too. She wanted to open the door again but she'd be damned if she was going to get into a who's-in-charge-here argument with him. She was in charge, and he would surely see a tussle over the ground rules as a sign of weakness.

Instead, she looked past him at the big clock above her work table.

"Ten seconds gone," she said briskly. "You're wasting time, your highness."

"What I have to say will take longer than five minutes."

"Then you'll just have to learn to economize. More than five minutes, I'll call the police."

Instantly, his hand was wrapped around her wrist. He tugged her toward him, his dark-chocolate eyes almost black with anger.

"You do that and I'll tell every tabloid shark I can contact about how Maria Santos tried to buy a five-hundred-thousand-dollar commission by seducing a prince." He smiled thinly. "They'll lap it up."

* * * * *

What will it take for this billionaire prince to realize he's falling in love with his mistress…?
Look for
BILLIONAIRE PRINCE, PREGNANT MISTRESS
by Sandra Marton
Available July 2009 from Harlequin Presents®.

We'll be spotlighting a different series every month throughout 2009 to celebrate our 60th anniversary.

Look for Harlequin® Presents in July!

TWO CROWNS, TWO ISLANDS, ONE LEGACY

A royal family, torn apart by pride and its lust for power, reunited by purity and passion

Step into the world of Karedes beginning this July with

BILLIONAIRE PRINCE, PREGNANT MISTRESS

by

Sandra Marton

Eight volumes to collect and treasure!

THE BELLES OF TEXAS

They're as strong as the state that raised them. The Belle sisters aren't afraid to go after what they want, whether it's reclaiming their ranch or their family.

Linda Warren
CAITLYN'S PRIZE

Thanks to her deceased father's gambling debts, Caitlyn Belle's beloved High Five Ranch is in dire straits. Particularly because the will stipulates that if the ranch doesn't turn a profit in six months, it must be sold to Judd Calhoun—the man Caitlyn jilted fourteen years ago. And Cait knows Judd has been waiting a long time for his revenge....

*Look for the first book
in The Belles of Texas miniseries,
on sale in July wherever books are sold.*

You're invited to join our Tell Harlequin Reader Panel!

By joining our new reader panel you will:

- Receive Harlequin® books—they are FREE and yours to keep with no obligation to purchase anything!
- Participate in fun online surveys
- Exchange opinions and ideas with women just like you
- Have a say in our new book ideas and help us publish the best in women's fiction

In addition, you will have a chance to win great prizes and receive special gifts! See Web site for details. Some conditions apply. Space is limited.

To join, visit us at
www.TellHarlequin.com.

REQUEST YOUR FREE BOOKS!

2 FREE NOVELS PLUS 2 FREE GIFTS!

SPECIAL EDITION®

Life, Love and Family!

YES! Please send me 2 FREE Silhouette Special Edition® novels and my 2 FREE gifts (gifts are worth about $10). After receiving them, if I don't wish to receive any more books, I can return the shipping statement marked "cancel." If I don't cancel, I will receive 6 brand-new novels every month and be billed just $4.24 per book in the U.S. or $4.99 per book in Canada. That's a savings of at least 15% off the cover price! It's quite a bargain! Shipping and handling is just 50¢ per book.* I understand that accepting the 2 free books and gifts places me under no obligation to buy anything. I can always return a shipment and cancel at any time. Even if I never buy another book from Silhouette, the two free books and gifts are mine to keep forever.

235 SDN EYN4 335 SDN EYPG

Name _____ (PLEASE PRINT) _____

Address _____ Apt. # _____

City _____ State/Prov. _____ Zip/Postal Code _____

Signature (if under 18, a parent or guardian must sign) _____

Mail to the **Silhouette Reader Service:**
IN U.S.A.: P.O. Box 1867, Buffalo, NY 14240-1867
IN CANADA: P.O. Box 609, Fort Erie, Ontario L2A 5X3

Not valid to current subscribers of Silhouette Special Edition books.

Want to try two free books from another line?
Call 1-800-873-8635 or visit www.morefreebooks.com.

* Terms and prices subject to change without notice. Prices do not include applicable taxes. Sales tax applicable in N.Y. Canadian residents will be charged applicable provincial taxes and GST. Offer not valid in Quebec. This offer is limited to one order per household. All orders subject to approval. Credit or debit balances in a customer's account(s) may be offset by any other outstanding balance owed by or to the customer. Please allow 4 to 6 weeks for delivery. Offer available while quantities last.

Your Privacy: Silhouette is committed to protecting your privacy. Our Privacy Policy is available online at www.eHarlequin.com or upon request from the Reader Service. From time to time we make our lists of customers available to reputable third parties who may have a product or service of interest to you. If you would prefer we not share your name and address, please check here. ☐

SSE09R

COMING NEXT MONTH

Available June 30, 2009

#1981 THE TEXAS BILLIONAIRE'S BRIDE—Crystal Green
The Foleys and the McCords
For Vegas showgirl turned nanny Melanie Grandy, caring for the daughter of gruff billionaire Zane Foley was the perfect gig...until she fell for him, and her secret past threatened to bring down the curtain on her newfound happiness.

#1982 THE DOCTOR'S SECRET BABY—Teresa Southwick
Men of Mercy Medical
It was no secret that Emily Summers had shared a night of passion with commitment-phobe Dr. Cal Westen. But she kept him in the dark when she had their child. Would a crisis bring them together as a family...for good?

#1983 THE 39-YEAR-OLD VIRGIN—Marie Ferrarella
It wasn't easy when Claire Santaniello had to leave the convent to teach and take care of her sick mother. Luckily, widowed father and vice detective Caleb McClain was there for her as she found her way in the world...and into his arms.

#1984 HIS BROTHER'S BRIDE-TO-BE—Patricia Kay
Jill Jordan Emerson was engaged to a wealthy businessman several years her senior—until she came face-to-face with his younger brother Stephen Wells, a.k.a. the long-lost father of her son! Now which brother would claim this bride-to-be as his own?

#1985 LONE STAR DADDY—Stella Bagwell
Men of the West
It was a simple case of illegal cattle trafficking on a New Mexico ranch, and Ranger Jonas Redman thought he had the assignment under control—until the ranch's very single, very pregnant heiress Alexa Cantrell captured his attention and wouldn't let go....

#1986 YOUR RANCH OR MINE?—Cindy Kirk
Meet Me in Montana
When designer Anna Anderssen came home to Sweet River, she should have known she'd run right into neighboring rancher Mitchell Donovan, the one man who could expose the secrets—and reignite passions—that made her run in the first place!

SSECNMBPA0609